DANE

A DADDIES MC NOVEL

LUCKY MOON

Content copyright © Lucky Moon. All rights reserved. First published in 2021.

This book may not be reproduced or used in any manner without the express written permission of the copyright holder, except for brief quotations used in reviews or promotions. This book is licensed for your personal use only. Thanks!

Disclaimer: This is a work of fiction. Names, characters, businesses, places, events, locales, and incidents are either the products of the author's imagination or used in a fictitious manner. Any resemblance to actual persons, living or dead, or actual events is purely coincidental.

Cover Image © Curaphotography Fotolia, Adobe Stock. Cover Design, Lucky Moon.

Table of Contents

DANE 1
CHAPTER ONE 5
CHAPTER TWO 13
CHAPTER THREE 21
CHAPTER FOUR 29
CHAPTER FIVE 39
CHAPTER SIX 47
CHAPTER SEVEN 55
CHAPTER EIGHT 63
CHAPTER NINE 71
CHAPTER TEN 81
CHAPTER ELEVEN 91
CHAPTER TWELVE 101
CHAPTER THIRTEEN 109
CHAPTER FOURTEEN 117
CHAPTER FIFTEEN 127
CHAPTER SIXTEEN 135
CHAPTER SEVENTEEN 143
CHAPTER EIGHTEEN 153
CHAPTER NINETEEN 161
CHAPTER TWENTY 171
CHAPTER TWENTY-ONE 179
CHAPTER TWENTY-TWO 187
CHAPTER TWENTY-THREE 195
CHAPTER TWENTY-FOUR 201
CHAPTER TWENTY-FIVE 209
CHAPTER TWENTY-SIX 219
CHAPTER TWENTY-SEVEN 227
CHAPTER TWENTY-EIGHT 233
CHAPTER TWENTY-NINE 237
NEXT IN SERIES 245
MORE FROM LUCKY MOON 246

CHAPTER ONE

HARPER

Why today? Of all the days, in all the weeks, in all the months, in all the years of my life, why did I have to get a fever today?

Decorating cakes is equal parts art and science, but today I don't feel either an artist or a scientist.

I just feel like a mess.

Come on Harper, concentrate. You can do this.

I slot my piping bag into a glass, before loading it up with buttercream, squishing the thick, sweet paste all the way to the bottom of the bag. Even this simple maneuver is an effort today. Everything's making me feel woozy. Buttercream oozes over the lip of the bag and plops down onto the work surface below. I let out a gasp of annoyance and wipe it up with a paper towel.

So. Much. Effort.

'OK, time to get piping!' I say, glancing up at Pudding. He's sitting on the windowsill, watching me silently. Mind you, it would be kinda weird if my stuffie said something about my cake decorating skills. Or about anything, for that matter.

Mind you, the way I feel right now, I'm half expecting to start hallucinating.

I squeeze a dollop of buttercream down onto the cake base, to secure the first layer of moist sponge. Normally, I'd be tasting the frosting at every possible opportunity. But today, even the thought of the super-sweet stuff is making me feel green around the gills.

'I hope this tastes as good as it looks,' I say, as I squeeze out a ring of buttercream around the edge of the circle of sponge, and then slowly fill in the center. 'Looks kinda like a snail shell, Pudding,' I say. 'A cute lil' cakey snail.'

Oh my gosh! I should totally make a snail cake. Snails are kinda my spirit animal. Small. Slow. Cute. Slimy.

OK, I'm not slimy, but maybe I'm those other words.

Well I guess maybe *sometimes* I'm slimy. But not always. Not snail slimy, anyways. Just regular slimy. Human slimy. This is gross.

'Harper, that cake isn't gonna decorate itself, Babygirl!'

I glance up at Pudding. He's still just sitting on the windowsill, not moving or talking. But it *sounded* like he spoke.

My head is rhythmically pounding with every single heartbeat. Feels like someone's cracking my skull with a hammer in time with my pulse. I know that Pudding didn't really speak, it's just my imagination. After all, cake-shaped soft toys with big googly eyes can't talk. Everyone knows that.

Even at the best of times, my imagination is a little bit wild. I think that's why I never did so well at school. It's not that I'm dumb — although I don't consider myself smart — but I just always found concentrating to be impossible. How are you meant to solve simultaneous equations when you could be day-dreaming about cartoon characters replacing all your teachers? How are you meant to analyze the language of Herman Melville when you could be imagining swimming alongside a pink whale off the coast of Madagascar?

How are you meant to decorate a cake, when you could be having a make-believe conversation with your stuffie?

'No, no, no!' I say, trying to snap myself out of my fever-induced dream. 'Harper needs to work!'

I stack the second layer of sponge, pipe in a new layer of buttercream, then add the final layer of cake. Now it's time to crumb-

CHAPTER ONE

coat the cake. That's a thin layer of frosting which goes all over it, to stop the cake drying out, and seal in all the crumbs. I refill the piping bag and splurge a load of it out over the sides of the cake, before starting to turn the now bright-pink cylinder on the cake board.

As I turn the cake, I smooth the frosting with a large scraper, making a solid, even, finish. This part of the process is so important and so easy to get wrong that I have to fully concentrate. I feel my tongue poking out, as my brow furrows with effort.

There's good reason for my concentration: this is probably the most important cake I've ever decorated in my life. I work for one of the biggest cake-baking and decorating companies in LA. Superstar Frosting is world famous. Set up by 'baker-to-the-stars' Frank Lamont in the late nineties, we provide themed cakes to all the biggest movie studios in Hollywood. If a movie-star needs a cake for a birthday party, or another special occasion, chances are, it'll be one of our cakes.

I first started working for Superstar Frosting about six months ago. I always dreamed of baking fabulous cakes for a living — it's kinda the one thing in life that I've been able to concentrate on for more than about five minutes — so when a position working as Frank Lamont's personal assistant came up, I jumped at the chance.

Sure — the job didn't involve any baking to begin with, and I've basically been working as Frank's personal slave since I started, but I've finally been given the opportunity of a lifetime: bake, decorate and deliver a cake for a party at the TCL Chinese Theater — Hollywood's most famous movie institution.

'And now, it's time to get serious.' I don't know why, but I'm talking like Arnie in Terminator right now. You know, a horrendous, possibly-offensive, definitely-annoying version of his voice. I whip up another batch of buttercream, this time, colored a lurid red. I'm delivering the cake to the premier of a slasher movie (definitely not the kind of movie I normally like to watch!) so I'm going for a super-gory vibe. The idea is to have a royal-frosting ax bursting through the side of the cake, between two layers of the red buttercream.

This is gonna be tricky, not to mention risky, but Frank's words keep ringing around my head like an angry bell.

'You fuck this up, and you'll be doing nothing but cake deliveries for the rest of your career.'

Yeah, turns out that Frank's kind of an asshole. I mean, he's a genius, but he's also an asshole. When I said that I've basically been his slave for six months, I was only exaggerating a teensy little bit. He's had me delivering cakes, getting him coffee, making up frosting, buying groceries — all the crappy jobs. And the pay has been virtually non-existent.

That's why I'm stuck in this crappy apartment. Honestly, calling it an apartment is generous. Pigsty is more like it. It's basically all kitchen. That's good in some ways — I need a big kitchen space for my baking — but it's never nice to sleep in the same place that you eat, and cook, and watch TV, and basically do everything.

Not only is this place tiny, it's also in one of the more — how do I put this — *rustic* parts of LA. I'm kinda halfway between Downtown and the Fashion District. About the nicest thing you can say about this part of town is that it's mostly safe. In the daytime. If you stick to the safe parts. And you're not a woman.

That's a mild over-exaggeration, but it is kind dodgy round here. My friend, Felicity, who lives a couple blocks away was mugged just a month ago. She hadn't been hurt, thankfully, but still, it was real scary hearing her story. It had happened in broad daylight, only a couple streets from her place. Trouble is gangs around here. You've got pushers

CHAPTER ONE

and pimps, hookers and bikers, and the cops basically won't step foot in the place. If you believe some people, the cops are just as bad as the gang-bangers. I don't know what to believe though.

I open up my fridge, take out the frosting ax that's been (literally) chilling in there for a day. I decided to make it in advance, something I'm really grateful for right now. Oohhh it's so cool in the fridge, I wanna crawl in and have a little sleep. Under normal circumstances, I'd be in bed right now, sleeping like a tiny little sloth. But today that's not an option.

Soon, the ax is fixed to the side of the cake and I'm ready for the final layer of frosting. Suddenly, I'm full of hope. Maybe this is gonna be alright. I pipe the frosting on evenly, and then, I brandish my scraper like it's an actual ax. I'm about to start smoothing off the red, when there's a knock at my door.

Huh. Who can that be? I'm not expecting any deliveries. I anxiously glance at my watch. 11:30. I'm due to deliver the cake in an hour and a half. So long as this isn't anything too weird, I should be able to get there on time.

'Coming!' I shout out, before washing my hands and giving myself a quick look in the mirror.

Well, I look like a rat that's been attacked by another, bigger, soaking-wet rat. Sweat has plastered my dark red hair to my forehead, and my cheeks are bright pink with the fever. My eyes — normally big and bright blue — are kinda squinty and puffy. I splash my face with cold water in the pathetic hope that it'll somehow make me look better but — guess what — it doesn't.

I pull the chain out of the lock, and tug the door open. It squeals as it reveals a hulking figure. He has to be six foot four or something, and he's dressed from head to toe in the most ridiculous collection of leathers I've ever seen. His face is stubbly, and he's wearing an over-size pair of aviator sunglasses, that would dwarf any normal face. But this isn't a normal face — it's heavy-set and pink, somehow threatening and comical at the same time.

'Well hello Little Lady.' His voice has a southern tang — I can't quite place it, but he's definitely not from LA originally.

'Hello?'

'I'm your new building manager.' He snorts, clears his throat, and then, to my disgust, spits something out onto the floor just outside my front door. I stifle the urge to retch, and I'm reeling from the rudeness and his aggressive behavior.

'You're my new building manager?' I ask, my voice uncertain.

'You're a quick study,' he replies, his voice cold, cruel. 'Smells fuckin' good in here,' he says, sniffing the air.

'What happened to Mrs. Anderson?' I want to keep on topic. I've got a schedule to stick to.

'Yeah, Miss Andrews is dead now.' He snorts again. I can't see his eyes, but I get the distinct impression that he's looking around the inside of my apartment. Scanning it for valuables. This guy really doesn't feel like a building manager.

'Do you have any credentials?' I say. I'm being way braver than I normally would be. I think that the fever's talking really, not me.

'I've got really fucking big credentials,' he says, smiling a nasty smile. 'But I don't think you'd wanna see them, sweetheart.'

Hmm, that might be something we actually agree on. I don't know what to say, but I feel my cheeks burn even brighter than they were a second ago. I don't say a word.

'Anyway, that's enough flirtin'. Don't wanna cross any lines.' He holds a finger up to my cheek — he reeks of smoke. He strokes me just

CHAPTER ONE

for a second, then, suddenly, he pulls it away. 'Look, I'm just here to warn you that I'm bringing in a new charge. A security charge. All the gangs in the area are causing trouble, see. So, I'm having to install a security system. I have to pass on the cost to my tenants, much as it pains me too.'

He doesn't look pained. In fact, he looks pretty happy with the situation.

'How much?' I ask. I'm feeling faint now, like all the blood is draining away from my head.

'Not much. For someone like you, I think,' he strokes his chin a second, 'About $150 a month. How does that sound.'

Sounds like you just plucked a random figure outta your butt, is what I *don't* say.

'I don't think I can afford that,' I say, quietly.

'I'm sure you'll find a way,' he says, eying my sternly. 'Or I'll find someone else who will.'

Is this guy who I've only just met threatening to kick me out of my apartment?

'I don't get it,' I say. Almost feels like my visions getting blurry now. Are there two men in front of me, or just one.

The guy standing in front of me looks me up and down slowly. 'Oh, you'll get it,' he says. Then he slowly — purposefully — licks his fat lips. For a horrible second, I think he's going to do something terrible. But instead, he turns and leaves. As he walks away, I see a huge patch stitched to the back of his leather jacket. Red letters on a white background: Blood Fuckers MC.

He turns back. 'I'd get some better locks if I were you. There are bad guys around here. The kind of guy who could smash that puny door of yours in half a second.' Then, he's gone.

LUCKY MOON

My anxiety builds My heart's pounding harder than it's ever pumped before.

Somehow, I need to finish this cake. Don't worry about the $150 I have no chance of ever paying. Don't worry about the fact that some kind of biker thug knows where I live and that my front door's about as strong as paper.

Never mind all that. I've got frosting to fix.

I don't know how, but even with my hands shaking and sweat pouring from my brow, I manage to get the frosting on even and smooth. The cake looks OK. No, it looks more than OK. Considering the situation, it looks damn-near perfect. I snap a photo of it for my own records, then I package it up into a big white box, printed with the Superstar Frosting logo. The final touch is a bright red ribbon, tied round the whole thing.

There's no way Frank could be disappointed with this, no way he'll be able to make me just a delivery-girl after this cake.

As I make my way down the concrete staircase to the bike-shed, I keep my eyes open for any sign of the biker-dude from before. Luckily, he's nowhere to be seen. I try to be extra careful with the cake — I don't want anything to spoil my hard work. I've got a rusty old bicycle — it's pale blue with a big basket on the front — and really it needs new tires and a new seat, but obviously right now I can't afford anything. I breathe a sigh of relief as I see that the cake box fits perfectly into the basket, but just to be doubly sure, I secure the bulky thing with a couple bungee cords.

I pull on my helmet and kick away from the kerb. It's a sunny day, and the sky is that pale LA blue that kind make even the shittiest neighborhood seem glamorous and beautiful. As I get up to speed, I get this weird feeling, like everything's gonna be alright.

CHAPTER TWO

DANE

Everything is fucked. I'm fucked. The club's fucked. This fucking city's fucked. And this traffic? Don't even get me started on this damn traffic.

Even though I'm on my hog, it's still virtually impossible to weave between all the angry cars and growling pick-ups that have clogged up this stretch of LA.

In theory, I'm only half an hour away from The Milk Shed, the bar I own. As well as one of the top drinking establishments in LA, it also happens to be the headquarters of my club. But in practice, with this fucking traffic, well, I could be stuck here for the better part of an hour. Angry and frustrated, I rev my bike, making an angry sputter of sound. It's childish, I know, but sometimes the only appropriate reaction to a crappy situation is a nice dose of petulance.

'Shut the fuck up!' I hear the cry from in front. A guy's stuck his head out the window of his sleek, German saloon car. He's giving me the finger. 'Stupid fucking biker prick! Shove that piece of trash bike up your ass!'

I see red, and before I know what I'm doing, my Harley's engine's growling like a wildcat between my legs, and I'm riding along the kerb to this asshole. As I approach, his arm retracts into the car and he starts to roll down the window. I pull up alongside and it's fully closed now.

I peer in — he's a skinny guy wearing the kind of round-circled spectacles that you might catch an accountant with. He's not so tough now that I'm next to his car, and in fact, he won't even catch my eye. I'm fuming, but I'm not gonna do anything over the top. Just put the fear of God into this asshole.

LUCKY MOON

Three sharp taps on his window. I see my reflection, my coarse beard, my hollow cheeks, my dark brown eyes, the scar on my cheek. As the window slides down, my face is replaced with his.

'Is there a problem?' he asks, his voice cracking slightly.

'You tell me.' I reply. My voice is steady, emotionless.

'No. No sir,' he almost stutters, but keeps it together.

'Well that's just dandy. See, the way you swore at me there, I almost thought we were gonna have a problem.'

'Swore at *you*?' He asks. I can practically see the sweat starting to form on his brow, can practically feel piss spread its way through his pants. 'No, no way! There was someone behind you, I thoug-'

'You're a lucky man,' I say, narrowing my eyes and cutting him off. 'If this were any other day, I'd probably have time to drag you out of that ugly-ass car of yours and teach you some manners. But today, I'm in a rush, so you get off lightly.' And without another word, I rev my bike again, for way longer than before, and I scoot off down the sidewalk.

Let me explain myself. I'd never *actually* hurt an asshole like that. I'm not a naturally violent person. Obviously, I can defend myself and the people I love, but I try to never be the aggressor. Thing is, I can't allow someone to insult my bike while I'm wearing club colors. It's part of the code, see? If he'd just insulted me, called me a prick, I wouldn't have even bothered talking to him. But the minute he called my beautiful Angeline a piece of trash, I had to take action.

'Good girl,' I say, patting the chrome of my hog with affection as we drive down the sidewalk. 'I'll always stick up for you, beautiful.'

She purrs back to me as I gun the throttle.

I know what you're thinking. What kind of maniac talks to his damn motorbike? What kind of maniac *names* his damn motorbike?

CHAPTER TWO

Well, the answer is: this maniac. Dane O'Brien. Vice President of Daddies MC, owner of the most gorgeous bike in LA, former criminal, current vigilante, lord of the fucking road. That's what kind of maniac I am.

I don't make a habit of driving on the sidewalk. It's pretty damn disrespectful, not to mention the fact that it's entirely illegal. But there's no one out on the sidewalk right now, and I'm in a hurry. It's a matter of life or death.

It's the first Monday of June, and every month, on the first Monday of the month, my Motorcycle Club meets. Normally, we just get half-cut and play a fuck of a lot of pool, but occasionally, we have business to discuss. Today's one of those rare days that the business on the table is so personally important to me that there's no way I can miss the meeting.

Most motorcycle clubs live an outlaw lifestyle. They're involved with gun-running, or drug-dealing, or people-smuggling, or all of the above. That's not the case with us though. Daddies MC is pretty much the opposite. I guess technically we *are* vigilantes. Don't go thinking Batman — although I guess we kinda dress similar. Some of us, at least.

We're more like a brotherhood that likes to protect our turf. We run legitimate businesses across central LA. My bar. Rock's tattoo parlor. Hawk's garage. And one very *specialist* nightclub. These types of business are all traditionally caught up in vice, in shady shit. So from time to time, we have to work together to drive out bad dudes from where we operate.

My phone starts to ring. I'm wearing a dumb-as-fuck bluetooth earpiece at the moment. I hate the way it looks and feels, but I can't afford to be disconnected from the club while I'm out riding.

Sometimes I long for the days of the past. No phones, no internet, no damn social media. Just the warm wind blowing over me as I ride my hog across this great country.

'This is Dane.'

'Where are you, bro?' I can just about hear Hawk's voice over the rumble of the engine.

'I'm on my fucking way.' I'm scanning the sidewalk for pedestrians. Clear for now.

'We're about to vote.'

'Sorry I'm late. Got caught in traffic.'

He sighs. 'You're gonna be the deciding vote, you know that right? We're split fifty-fifty on this fucking thing.'

My heart pounds in my chest. Fifty-fifty? I thought I had way more support than that. 'Damn it, Hawk, can you stall the vote for like, twenty minutes?'

'And you'll definitely be here in twenty?'

I curse under my breath. 'I definitely won't be longer than an hour.'

Hawk curses, but not under his breath. 'Fuck, Dane, what was so important that you couldn't just spend the morning here?'

Fuck if I'm gonna tell him that. 'I was just busy, alright?'

'Dane yo-' he sounds exasperated, but I just want to shut this down. I'm a private person, and I've got a reputation to maintain. If Hawk and the rest of the boys knew what I was up to this morning, I'd be a fucking laughingstock.

'I'm telling you to leave it, Hawk. I'll be quick as I can. Just stop the damn vote if you can.'

'No promises,' Hawk says, then he hangs up. It's not his fault, and in his position, I'd be pretty fucking annoyed, too. He and I are close, always have been. Probably feels hurt that I can't share my every move with him.

CHAPTER TWO

Fuck. I'm running out of sidewalk. I wrench my hog off the raised slabs and come to rest behind a white pick-up. It's traffic, as far as the eye can see. A shimmering haze of smog and sunlight stretches out in front of me. There's only one option, but it's not a great one. I'm gonna have to take a shortcut. Of course, by shortcut, what I mean is that I'm gonna take a much longer route, in the desperate hope that I can shave a couple minutes off my ETA.

Still, I'm not one to give my problems too much thought. Much more like me to make a quick decision, and stick to it. So, I wrench my handlebars to the right, and head down a smaller street. It's not exactly traffic free down here, but it's a damn sight better than on Alamena Street. I'm traveling back from Compton to the Fashion District. It's always a shitty drive, but this is fucking ridiculous.

I pick up a little speed, and clear my head.

For months now, there's been a drug problem in our turf. We don't know who is behind the recent surge in narcotics, and we don't know how the drugs are getting into the neighborhood. We run a pretty tight operation for the most part, stopping the flow of the majority of the narcotics before they can do any damage. We're not perfect, obviously — there's no way you can entirely stop people getting drugs into a part of LA — but we do a lot better than some neighboring districts.

Today, we're voting to see whether we go on the offensive. I want to start investigating, want to find out which gang's behind all this, and put them out of commission. Not everyone in the club shares my views though. Some of the more timid boys think that we should leave well enough alone, that we shouldn't poke our noses into other people's business. Not me though. Our club is meant to be all about protecting vulnerable people. That's the whole point of Daddies MC. If we don't stop this filth from flooding our streets, we're abandoning the people who need us most. And I'm not gonna let that happen. Not after what drugs did to me. Not after what they took away from me. And I think enough of us share my point of view. Now I just need to fucking get there.

I turn a corner, onto Grazia, and to my delight, the whole road is clear of traffic. Maybe I can make up some time, here. Maybe I've got a chance to get to the Milk Shed on time. I shift up a gear and gun the throttle, shooting down the center of the street, the wind suddenly battering my leather-covered chest.

There's a honk behind me, and for a second — no, less than a second — I glance down into my mirror to see if someone I know is trying to flag me down.

In that tiny fraction of time that I don't have my eyes on the road, disaster strikes. I feel a sickening crunch, and I let out a grunt of surprise. I don't come off my bike, but the person I've hit isn't so lucky. I see the bicycle first, spinning out across the street, the back wheel still turning as it comes to a halt. Something's come off the front of the bike and is smeared across the asphalt: a long, lurid smudge of red. Is that... cake? For a moment I'm so distracted by the fucking cake I forget to look at who I've hit. It's like I'm in a nightmare. Everything's moving slow and it feels like the only color I can see is that bright red streak.

Then, I feel my heart pound, and I come to my senses. That's when I see her: the most beautiful woman in the world.

Flowing out from beneath her bright pink helmet, a cascade of gorgeous auburn hair, in loose ringlets. Bright pink lips and pale, freckled cheeks.

And she's not moving.

Fuck fuck fuck.

I don't even turn my bike off, I just jump off and run to the poor

CHAPTER TWO

girl. Please be alive, please be alive.

I crouch down, push my face right next to hers, listen out for a breath and then, to my surprise, delight, and infinite annoyance, she says, 'You're ugly.'

'Well thank you, miss,' I grunt.

She blinks open her eyes, rubs her head. 'What happened?' She grabs at the strap at her chin and undoes the helmet. 'My head feels a bit hurty.'

My pride's still stinging from the ugly comment, but I'm not gonna dwell on it. She obviously needs my help.

'You came off your bike. It was my fault.'

'No no no,' she says. 'I had my eyes closed. Silly me!'

I'm getting a weird feeling from this girl. Like she's high or something. But then I see her forehead. It's dripping with sweat. I hold out my hand, press it against her skin. She's burning up.

'You've got a fever,' I say. 'I'm calling an ambulance.' I grab my phone.'

'No!' she says. 'No insurance. I can't and my cake needs to get to its home.'

'No insurance?' I scratch my head. Only one thing for it. There's no way I'm letting her ride home. She'll get killed. 'Fine. You're coming with me.'

'With you, Daddy?'

I'm stunned for a second. I know she doesn't mean it, I know she's delirious, but hearing that word come out of her lips does something strange to me. Like a part inside me has just been gripped and twisted, and it's left me changed forever.

'I'm gonna pick you up now, OK, Babygirl?' Is she a Little? Can't be. What are the chances that I'd literally ride into one?

LUCKY MOON

But she's got a pink helmet. Does that mean something?

Ugh. I'm such an idiot. Just because someone's wearing a damn item of pink clothing it doesn't mean they're a Little. Talk about wishful thinking.

She nods. I lean in, loop my arms around her waist. She reaches up, holds onto my neck. 'You're big. Really big. And ugly.' She giggles, then, as I easily lift her up, she adds, 'And really, really strong.'

With her in my arms, I walk over to the bike and pick it up. It's a rusted old thing, but once it was pretty enough. Still not putting the girl down, I grab a spare chain from the side pannier of my bike, then I padlock the rusted old bike to a post at the side of the road. I'll send someone to grab this later.

'No sir,' she says, slowly shaking her head.'

'It's easy. Hold onto me, and don't fall off.'

I plonk her down on the back of the Harley, and slide on in front of her. The bike's still idling, thrumming away beneath us.

'That feels funny,' she says, giggling like a schoolgirl as if to convince me. 'My you-know-what is tingling!'

Who is this woman, and what is she doing on my bike?

'Oh Babygirl, you're gonna regret this chat in the morning.' I twist my wrist, fire up my hog, and turn back towards my place.

And it's only when I pull up outside my home that I realize I'm gonna miss the vote. But the crazy thing is, when I help the girl off my bike and inside, it strikes me that I just don't care. Because I know that I'm doing the right thing.

CHAPTER THREE

HARPER

The first thing that strikes me, as I swirl up to consciousness, is that it smells really dang weird in here.

Good weird, but good. Leather and musk and another scent I can't quite pick out. I drift into wakefulness, and my heart flutters with a sudden spike of anxiety.

'Where am I?' the words pass my lips before I even have time to register speaking them. I try to lift myself up but stop and wince with pain — my head's throbbing, and I still feel feverish. In fact, almost as soon as I've stopped talking, my teeth start to chatter together like a crazy set of Halloween dentures.

I slump back down into the bed I'm on. My trembling body is covered in sheets and blankets. I'm warm enough, but I can't stop shivering. Just can't stop.

'Ripper, big man, she's up.' I recognize the voice, but I don't know who it belongs to. It's gruff, hard, cold, and really close-by. I blink my eyes open and look towards its source. When I see his face, I have to stop myself from screaming out. Burning eyes, an ugly scar on his cheek, lean and mean and full of fiery intensity. My eyes stray down to his body — he's wearing a tee shirt, tight across a massive torso. I can see every bulge and flex of his muscles underneath. Even though he's still, it looks as though his body is fighting to burst outta that shirt.

'Please don't hurt me!' My voice is so shrill and scared, I barely recognize myself.

But he doesn't react like I'm expecting to. There's no cruelty, no nasty smirk. His expression just softens, and he lifts a hand to my shoulder, squeezes gently. 'You're safe, Babygirl. I'm not gonna let anything bad happen to you. No fucking chance.'

Babygirl? Does he know, somehow? Am I that easy to read?

Looking at him, I'm lost. I follow the inky black of tattoos up his forearms and onto his rock-hard biceps: snaking dragons; gruesome skulls; a grinning, flaming, demon head.

'Who are you.'

'Dane,' he grunts, low and raspy, like a chain dragged across pumice.

'Where am I?'

I hear another voice. 'You're in the best damn free hospital this side of Beverly Hills, that's where.' I hear a door burst open, and another man enters the room. 'Is the patient lucid, Mr. O'Brien?'

'My name's Harper, not Lucy,' I say, mishearing.

'Move aside please,' says the second man to Dane. I guess he's called Ripper.

Ripper doesn't really look like someone who should be called Ripper. He's an older gentleman, with a bright white mustache, and dancing blue eyes. He's got on a pair of thick-rimmed glasses and this honestly really hipster-ish haircut: shaved at the sides, long on top, and white as snow.

'Look at the pen, please, sweetheart,' he says, holding up a fancy-looking fountain pen.

I do as I'm told as he moves it left and right, up and down. He seems to be really studying my face, watching my every move.

'Any pain anywhere in your body? Arms, legs?'

I shake my head. 'Just my head.'

'Probably dehydrated. Dane, grab a pitcher of water. Full, please.'

Dane ducks out and returns seconds later with a jug, before pouring me a tall glass. I gulp the liquid desperately. Feels like it's the first drink

CHAPTER THREE

I've had in weeks. I'm so eager that I feel some of the water pouring down my chin, soaking into the collar of my top.

'Looks like that hit the spot,' Dane says.

'I'm going to need to take your temperature now, young lady,' Ripper says. 'Now of course the most accurate way to tell temperature is by using an ana-'

'Ripper, I think a standard oral thermometer will be just fine,' Dane cuts in.

'What other type is there?' I ask, through a haze of feverish stupidity.

'Just don't worry about it,' Dane says. He crosses his thick arms in front of him, watches with an intensity I'm not used to.

Ripper pops a thermometer in my mouth, and while we wait for the reading, I try to take in some of my surroundings. I've never been in a room quite like this before. The walls are painted black. Like, who does that? Totally black walls? On the walls are huge, framed posters for bands I've vaguely heard of, but don't know much about. Judas Priest. Iron Maiden. Mastodon.

Then I look straight up. Above the bed is a huge set of antlers, poking into the room like a crazy pincushion.

Ripper pulls thermometer out my mouth and quickly looks at the gauge.

'Oh dear. One-oh-two point two. That's not a healthy temperature young lady.'

'I'm a bit ill,' I say.

'Definitely an illness?' Dane asks, a strange look on his face.

'For sure,' Ripper confirms. 'Nothing more sinister going on at all.'

Sinister? What's that meant to mean?

'She gonna be OK?' Dane presses. Is that genuine concern in his voice? Who is this guy, and why does he care about me?

'She's gonna be just fine.' Ripper stands up. He's dressed grungy, with a leather vest over a white tee, and a pair of oil-stained blue-jeans. Not your typical doctor look. He pulls out a little orange tub from inside a vest pocket. 'Give her two of these every four hours, and make sure that she drinks a fuck-ton of water.'

I'm suddenly struck by the weirdness of the situation. I don't know where I am. I don't know who these people are. And he's giving me something to take?

'Is it heroin?' I say. As soon as the words leave my mouth, it's obvious what a dumb question it is.

'Far more dangerous than that,' says Ripper, giving me a mischievous grin. 'This is one hundred percent pure Tylenol.'

'OK Rip, enough teasing, this poor girl needs some rest.'

Ripper nods, tosses the tub of pills to Dane, who confidently catches it. 'Don't worry, Dane, looking after this young lady should be a piece of cake.' And with that, he turns and leaves. It's only a few seconds after he's gone that something hits me. And it hits me so hard, it almost takes my dang head off.

Oh fuck. Cake. Fucking cake!

As soon as the memory comes to me, I feel ice in my veins, and the pain in my head doubles in intensity. But I don't care. I lurch up, pull the covers away from me, try desperately to find my feet. 'No, no, no,' I groan, as I wobble a little, finally managing to stand. 'I need to go, right now, I've got to deliver the cake to The Chinese Theater.'

'Woah there,' Dane says, swooping in so that he's supporting my weight. 'You're not going anywhere, young lady.'

'You can't keep me here.'

He sighs. 'Well, that's true enough. Got no intention of forcing you

CHAPTER THREE

against your will.'

'Then get out of my way and let me deliver my cake. I've only got until one to get it there.'

'Darling, what day do you think this is?'

'What day?' I can practically feel the color drain from my already pale cheeks. Have I really been here for a full day? 'It's Tuesday... right?'

He purses his lips. Shakes his head. 'It's Wednesday. You've been asleep for over 24 hours.'

'That can't be right. I don't even know how I got here. Did you put me to bed?'

'Nope. You demanded it.' He looks thoughtful, then says, 'If I remember correctly, your exact words were: Baby Harpy go beddy-byes now.'

The cold slap of embarrassment is just brutal. 'Oh my gosh, I'm so sorry.' Then it comes back — a vague memory of riding straight into his bike, of him scooping me up. Of me... oh no... I didn't.... 'I called you D-'

'You were out of it,' he says, saving me further embarrassment. 'Don't worry about all that stuff. I can't even remember what you were saying, anyway.'

I'm still standing, and he's supporting me. 'I'm in so much trouble,' I say. 'I'm gonna get fired.'

'Fired?' he says. He looks me in the eye. 'You can't get fired for being sick.'

'I can,' I reply. 'I'm not exactly in my boss's good books. I need my phone, I need to call him, apologize, do something to try and sort out his massive dog-poop I've landed in. I can't believe Frank's gonna fire me.'

'I could get your phone,' he says, looking at me tenderly. 'But you know what? If you're fired, you're fired. Can't get any more fired than fired, can you? So just forget about that job. Right now, you need to get better. Health is more important than anything else. So why don't you lie down, take a couple Tylenol, and tell me about your asshole boss?'

'Who the heck *are* you?' I ask, my brain feeling as frazzled as my body.

'Like I said, I'm Dane. Who I am isn't so important. Main thing is I'm gonna look after you 'til you don't need me any more. Then, if you want, you'll never see me again.'

This is crazy, but I kinda feel like I don't want to go anywhere. And in a way, he's right. If Frank's decided to fire me, there's not much I can do about it. Probably all I deserve as well. I'm not exactly good at arguing my case, either. Wouldn't be able to convince Frank to keep me on. Might as well just stay here.

'Are we still in LA?' I ask, my head throbbing again.

'Course. I'm not a kidnapper.' He grips his forehead, as though searching for the right words. 'Look, it's simple. When I saw you on the ground like that, I knew I had to help you. I felt guilty as fuck. Didn't have a choice. So. Now you're here.'

I get the impression that he's not really used to expressing himself. Maybe he's not used to talking to a girl, either.

'Well, thanks, I guess,' I say.

He lifts me up, and I'm reminded about the way he held me yesterday, the ease with which he'd moved me.

'Oh shit!' I say. 'I rode your bike.'

'You've got quite the mouth on you, don't you?' There's something about the way he says that.

'Yeah. Potty mouth. Sorry. I'm tryna' work on it.'

He slides me into the bed. 'Well, why don't I help you out with

CHAPTER THREE

that? While you're staying at mine, why don't we say that you're not allowed to swear?'

'Like a house rule?' I ask, as he pulls up the covers and tucks me in.

'Something like that.'

'What if I do though?' I ask. For some reason, I feel a little burst of excitement at the thought of what he might do.

'Oh I don't know,' he says. 'I'll tell you off.' Then he laughs, 'though I could always wash your mouth out, if you like.'

I bite my lip. 'Oh no,' I say, barely able to mask my excitement. 'That would be awful. Yuck.'

His eyes narrow, like he's trying to figure something out. 'Anyway, you won't have to deal with that unless you swear. Which you won't. Right, open wide.'

I look at him for a moment, trying to work out what he means.

'Your mouth, honey. Time for your medicine.' He unscrews the cap on the pill bottle and shakes a couple of the small, white capsules onto his hard, wide palm.

I open my mouth in a big 'o' and hold out my hand. He passes me the pills and I swallow them down, wincing at the slight bitter taste on my tongue. He gives me more water, and I wash the Tylenol down with a big mouthful, then I drag my hand across my mouth, wiping up and excess.

'Good girl,' he says. 'You're gonna be feeling better in no time.' Then, he does the strangest thing. He leans in, and for a moment, it almost looks like he's gonna stroke my head. But at the last minute, his hand changes course, and he ends up lightly punching me on my shoulder. 'Can't tell you how glad I am that you didn't get hurt in that accident. Never woulda forgiven myself.'

For the first time in days, I feel my fever lessen, just a tiny bit. It can't be the Tylenol. It might be the water.

Or maybe it's just the knowledge that right now, for this short moment, I'm in the exact right place. Even though I don't have the faintest idea where I am.

'Can I ask you a question?'

'Okie doke,' I say, forgetting myself.

'What's your name?'

I slip into the covers, and Dane arranges them gently around me.

'I'm Harper. Pleased to meet you.' I close my eyes.

'Harper, it's time to get some rest,' he says.

As I start to drift off, I have a naughty thought: I hope I don't get too well, too soon.

He turns and moves to leave. And as he does, on the back of his t-shirt, I see letters: DADDIES MC. Underneath is a grinning white skull. A chill runs up and down my spine, then, before I have a chance to freak out, I'm asleep, gentle and sure as a baby.

CHAPTER FOUR

DANE

I don't know whether to be proud of myself, or furious at what I've done.

Always thinking with your dick, Dane.

I wonder if that's true. Was I thinking with my dick when I decided to abstain from the most important vote in the history of Daddies MC to save a hot girl? Or was I thinking with my heart?

That's all academic, anyway, cause we lost the fucking vote. Hawk's furious with me, of course. He's got past issues with drugs, too, so he was devastated when he learned I wasn't gonna make it.

'You've made your damn choice now, Dane, you're gonna have to live with it.' I've got a feeling that his words are gonna be with me for a while.

I crack the egg in my hand with so much force that shards of shell fall into the bowl, alongside the yolk and white.

'Fucksake,' I swear, picking the fragments out as best I can. But there's too much. I pour the egg away and start over. 'Can't make an omelet without obliterating a few eggs,' I grunt wryly, then I wince as my back twinges with pain. Harper's been with me for almost two days now, and I've been sleeping on the couch the whole time. It's not exactly ergonomic.

Still, it's worth it. Even though I don't know Harper basically at all, I get this feeling from her. Like she's a good person. A heck of a better person than I am. I'll sleep on the couch every day for the rest of my life if people like her can be comfortable and healthy.

I'm glad I got Rip to come and look her over. Good to set my mind at ease. Plus, I wanted to make sure that she wasn't just high. I don't have a problem with addicts — in my opinion they're victims — but I wanna know where I stand with people. Don't want to be wondering why Tylenol isn't fixing a raging physical withdrawal from smack.

Last night, she woke for about twenty minutes, and I managed to get some chicken noodle soup down her, but this morning I need to make sure that she eats something really nutritious and packed full of calories. Her body's fighting an infection, and it needs fuel. Huevos rancheros. Everyone loves huevos rancheros, right?

I'm about to crack a second egg into a fresh bowl, when my phone starts to buzz.

Thank fuck. I've been waiting for this call for nearly twenty-four hours. I wipe my hand on a dishcloth and answer the call.

'This is Dane.'

'Why have I got forty fucking missed calls from this number on my phone?' An angry, impatient voice. Full of irritation, with a whiny note that I wasn't expecting.

'Frank, I take it?'

'How did you get this number. It's my private phone. Work queries are meant t-'

'Never mind that. I want to talk to you about your employee, Harper.'

It was actually quite easy to find out his mobile number. Especially when you know as many shady figures as I do. Soon as Harper mentioned the Chinese Theater, it was only a matter of time, and a couple of innocent phone calls, before I discovered the name of the bakery she works for.

'I think you mean my ex-employee.' He lets out a smarmy laugh. Well, you seem great.

CHAPTER FOUR

'You know she was involved in an accident recently?'

'An accident?' Hard to read him from his tone of voice. Never spoken to someone as defensive as this fucker. What's his deal?

'That's right. A road accident. And on top of that, she's sick. She was sick on the day she was meant to deliver your cake. Did you know that?'

'No,' he says, sounding flustered. 'But that's her problem. You get sick, you work through it. She's a grown woman, not a baby.'

'That's your philosophy, is it?'

'Who the fuck are you? Her dad? Her boyfriend?'

'Doesn't matter. I take it now you know she was sick you're not gonna fire her?' I crack another egg, successfully this time.

He lets out a bark of laughter. 'Get fucked, idiot.'

'Well, in that case I'm afraid I'm gonna have to raise a suit against you, based on section four, sub-section three of the family and medical leave act.'

He pauses, lets what I've said sink in.

'She can't afford a lawyer.'

I'm not gonna argue with him. Just gonna steamroller this whiny asshole. 'Here's what you're gonna do. When she calls you and begs you for her job, you're gonna pretend you haven't heard from me. Chew her out, do whatever you'd normally do, but don't fire her.'

'A lawyer wouldn't be calling me, either. This is bullsh-'

'My friend,' I say, as unfriendly as I can manage, 'You're right. I'm not a lawyer. I'm far, *far* fucking worse than that. I'm your worst nightmare. And unless you want a very *intimate* encounter with Freddy fucking Krueger, you'll do as I say.'

He pauses for a moment. I can hear his breathing — heavy, rasping. Sounds overweight. Makes sense, for the head of a luxury baking brand.

I hear him swallow. Then, resigned, he says, 'Ugh. Fine. Whatever. I won't fire her.'

'Good.'

'Is that it? Anything else?'

I can't help but smile. 'I think you should thank me. I just saved you a fortune in legal fees.'

'Go to hell.' The phone cuts out. Maybe I shouldn't have pushed him like that. But I didn't like the way he spoke to me. And I didn't like the way he spoke about Harper. I feel insanely protective about her, and it's kinda weird.

She called me Daddy. Never been called that before.

My club was born out of a shared interest. Bud, the president, runs a BDSM club called The Nursery in Downtown LA. It's where Daddies MC was founded, over a decade ago. Most, if not all of the members are members of the age play community. Thing is, I've never really thought of myself as a Daddy. Nope. My path into the club was a little more complicated, and a lot messier.

Since I met Harper though… it's like something's woken up in me. Like some latent personality is bubbling up. And I don't even know if I feel like myself any more.

'Hello?!' A soft, quiet, inquisitive voice. Harper's up. I thought I heard her stirring a couple minutes ago. Hope she didn't hear me on the phone too clearly.

'Glad to hear you're up.'

A moment later, I hear footsteps padding into the kitchen.

'I feel better!' Good — surely she would have mentioned it if she realized I was on the phone to Frank.

I turn to look at her. She *looks* better. No — scratch that. She looks *incredible*.

CHAPTER FOUR

Her dark auburn hair falls to her shoulders, her bright blue eyes sparkle. The smattering of freckles across her nose and cheeks look like dim stars in the night sky. She's wearing one of my t-shirts, and it's massive on her, but even the baggy, shapeless black thing can't hide her incredible body — the sweep of those breasts, the tightness of her waist, her generous, curvaceous hips. I feel a tug of lust at my groin. Fuck. I'm actually into this fucking girl.

I swallow. 'Glad to hear it.' My voice sounds slightly strangled, but I manage to hide the fact that I'm basically drooling. 'Got breakfast, if you want it.'

She peeks round me.

'Looks like an uncooked egg in a bowl.'

'It's my specialty. Huevos Bowleros.'

She giggles, and it's just about the sweetest sound I've ever heard. 'I haven't had that before. Bet it's delicious.'

'Why don't you take a seat at the breakfast bar.' I gesture with a spatula towards a tall chair at the other end of the kitchen.

She makes a funny noise, then heads to the chair. 'Weird that a guy like you has a breakfast bar.'

'Oh? What kind of guy do you think I am?' I turn my attention to the cooking.

'I dunno. Um. Wow. I guess I'm a jerk.' Her cheeks visibly pinken with embarrassment.

Can't help but laugh. 'No, you're not. I get it. I'm big. Maybe scary-looking. I get it. I'm just pulling your leg.' I don't wanna make her feel bad. 'Truth is, I didn't choose the breakfast bar. It came with the place.'

'Like what you've done with it.' She looks around at the walls, at my posters and prints. 'Very... gothic?'

'If you say so.' I whisk the eggs together. It's amazing. She doesn't seem to be anxious. Doesn't seem to want her phone, or to get out of here. Does she like being here? Being with me? No. That's just wishful thinking on my part.

'Dane?'

'Yeah?'

'What's Daddies MC?'

The question takes me by surprise. 'Where did you hear about Daddies MC?'

'Saw it on your t-shirt yesterday. Is it some TV show I haven't seen?'

'Nope.' Damn my fucking honesty. Sometimes, it would be so much easier to lie. But I just can't do it. 'It's a club. Motorbikes.'

'You're a biker?'

'Didn't the ride on my bike tip you off?'

It looks like she's just seen the sunrise for the first time. 'Holy shit! I drove on a damn motorbike! I totally forgot!'

Hmmm. She swore. Should I call her out on it? Would she like it? Am I crazy to be even thinking about this?

My heart pounds, then I decide to take a risk. 'Hey, was that a cuss word?'

Somehow, her mouth stretches even wider, then she slaps both her hands over it, in a gesture of shame and surprise.

'I forgot! Oh no! I'm sorry!' The way she talks — so cute, with an upward inflection on her sentences — it's like she's screaming at me that she's a Little. Not my type. Least, it never has been before.

I shake my head. 'Sorry won't cut it, I'm afraid.'

She looks genuinely terrified. 'What are you gonna do?'

'Don't worry. First time's only a tiny little punishment. Nothing too bad.'

'No spanking?'

CHAPTER FOUR

I pause, lay my hands on either side of the Huevos Bowleros. 'Harper, can I ask you something?'

She nods.

'Are you a Little?'

Mouth closed. Eyes wide. 'What do you me-'

'You know what I mean.' My voice comes out more serious than I mean. Almost... angry. But I'm not. In fact, the last thing I want is for her to be scared, to close up to me. I just feel so sure about this. If she's not a Little then I'm not an ugly bastard.

She takes a moment. Purses her lips.

'Sorry,' I say. 'Not trying to be mean. I know this is hard to talk about. It's just... first there was the sparkly pink helmet. Th-'

'Everyone wears pink helmets!'

'Well, not everyone, but I take your point. I think the thing that really made me suspect was the fact you called me Daddy.'

A look of horror on her gorgeous face. I feel for her, I really do.

'Um. I think I better go.'

It's not the answer I expected. But I get it. I made a mistake.

'Sure.' I say. 'Of course. You must have stuff to get on with.'

'Yeah,' she says, quietly.

Can't believe things were going so well, then I fucked them up so badly.

'Gonna have to give you something to eat though. I can't have you leave without any food. You're liable to collapse. Plus, you need your Tylenol. Promise I won't talk about Little stuff. Just need to get you fueled up.'

She looks at me with gratitude.

'I *am* hungry. Like, really, really hungry.'

'Well, do you want eggs, or cake?'

'Or both?' she gives me a mischievous grin.

'Or both,' I concede.

*

As she tears into eggs, then cake, we make small talk. I tell her about my bar, she tells me about her dream to be a baker. The more we talk, the more certain I am that she's a Little. She's got that same combination of wide-eyed wonder, scatterbrained cuteness, and over-excitement that I see in the Littles of the other club members.

Obviously, she's not interested in sharing that part of herself with me. I can respect that.

I know what I look like: a scarred, gruff brute. I must be twice her age, too. She's such a sweetheart, and so fucking gorgeous that she could have just about anyone she wanted. No way she'd want someone like me.

Eventually, as she wipes the crumbs from her mouth, I say, 'I've got something for you.'

'Something else? You've been so generous already.'

'Well, this is kinda yours already, so…'

'I'm intrigued.'

'Don't get too excited.' I stand, gesture to the door. 'Into the hallway, please.'

When she sees what I've got waiting for her, she squeals with delight.

'Is that *my bike*?'

'Yep. Same bike.'

It admittedly looks a hell of a lot better than it did a couple days ago. In fact, it's barely recognizable. Gone is the rust and the old chain that

CHAPTER FOUR

was almost worn through. Gear cogs have been replaced, and we even fixed up the saddle.

'How did you-'

'My club owns a garage. Obviously, we mostly do motorbikes, but, it's the same principle.'

She turns to look at me, clasps her hands together. 'How can I ever repay you?'

'Just look where you're pedaling, kiddo.' I grin.

'You've been so kind.'

'Nah. Don't mention it.'

Is that a tear running down her face?

'Oh, before I forget, here's your phone,' I hand it over. 'I've kept it switched off. Just do me a favor and wait til you get home before you make any calls.'

She nods. Then, before I can stop her, she launches herself at me. She pushes her chest into mine, wraps her arms round me. I feel the soft fullness of her breasts, I smell the soft vanilla scent of her skin. She squeezes, before she pulls back.

Then, she opens my front door, and steps into the sun, and out of my life.

CHAPTER FIVE

HARPER

Why did I have to cuddle him? Why did I have to push myself up against him like that?

He felt so good. He *smelled* so good. Dang. He smelled like some kinda powerful beast — musky and salty, with this clean, citrus tang. The effect his body had on mine was instant. I felt a tightening and warmth start to spill from the place between my legs. That's why I pulled away so quick — because if I'd stayed that close to him for even a second more, I might have done something seriously dumb.

I can't forget that feeling though. Can't shake off the memory of his scent. I'm tingling, buzzing, practically vibrating on my cycle home. My bike feels totally different now — it's like he's bought me a whole new machine. I can actually *feel* the oil on the chain and the new gears. I know it sounds stupid.

I wish that I didn't feel embarrassed about being a Little. I wish I hadn't frozen up when he'd asked me. But I did. And I do.

Maybe I'll never get over what happened to me at school. Just thinking about it makes me feel yucky and sad. Maybe I'll never shake off that feeling of humiliation and shame. It's so bad that even the thought of anyone knowing that I'm a Little makes me feel a kind of prickly panic that's actually making me feel nauseous.

No one knows. Not my parents. Not my best friend Felicity. Not anyone. And that's the way it's gonna stay.

Except he knows, Harper. Dane knows.

I hate that voice. My doubt, my worry. My shame.

Speaking of which...

LUCKY MOON

Since staying at Dane's place, I've been kinda avoiding thinking about my job, and about Frank. I'm actually really good at ignoring bad stuff. Sometimes it can work in my favor — when I need to just focus on something — but more often than not, it leads to me procrastinating. I avoid my problems, which I know can't be good.

It's such a lovely sunny day, and it feels like nothing bad can happen to me when it's sunny. But I know it's not true.

As I start to get closer to my place, I almost feel like there's a dark cloud forming over me. It's the thought of facing up to reality. Of talking to Frank. Of most likely getting fired. I don't know what my plan will be if I *do* actually lose my job. No way I'll be able to keep up with the rent payments, let alone pay this ridiculous new 'security fee'. The more I start to wallow in the bleakness of my situation, the more sad and depressed I get, until just as I'm about to turn the corner on my street, it feels as though the sky's about to fall and crush me.

I sigh deep, and turn the corner.

There's my place. I could go in. Make a call to Frank. Beg him over the phone to let me keep my job.

But I'm desperate, and desperate times call for desperate measures.

I turn my new-old bike around and head into the center of LA.

*

'Oh my God, the prodigal child returns!' Blake is piping something very blue onto the top of a triple-layer celebration cake.

'Nice to see you too,' Blake.

The interior of the front of Superstar Frosting is half industrial bakery, half boutique patisserie. There's a counter, next to huge, glass-fronted fridges full of incredible-looking cakes and pastries. We're

CHAPTER FIVE

particularly famous for Tarte Au Citron — one of my favorite deserts.

'You're in so much trouble!'

Blake is one of the best bakers here. He's a good guy, dedicated to his craft, and a super-hard worker. He finishes a line of the blue frosting, and stands back to admire his handiwork.

'You don't need to tell me that.' I unstrap my helmet. 'I'm basically toast.'

'You're brave, coming in.' Blake's got big brown eyes, with some of the longest eyelashes I've ever seen. I used to joke with him that he should get hairnets just for his eyes. You know, back in the days when I actually felt like joking.

'Is Frank in?' I guess I'm half-hoping that he's not. I decided that coming in here is my best chance of keeping my job. But I'm not kidding myself. My chances of survival are slim to none.

'You bet.'

'I don't suppose he's in a good mood, is he?'

Blake grins and shakes his head. 'He was. Then he took a phone call about an hour ago, which sent him berserk. Hasn't come out of his office since.'

Oh, that's a bad sign. Frank likes to be out in the bakery, watching over his bakers' shoulders as they finish their decorations, dolling out criticism like candy.

'Great.'

Blake reaches out a blue-gloved hand and squeezes my arm. 'Don't worry honey, you're gonna be fine. Remember, you're a talented baker. Don't let Frank have you believe otherwise.'

He's a sweetheart, and I appreciate his encouragement, but I don't feel much better. Truth is that Blake's never actually watched me bake and decorate a cake. Frank said I wasn't allowed to work here with the others. After months of pestering, he finally let me bake a cake for him, as a test. I took it round his house, and he examined it for five minutes before cutting into it with a sharp kitchen knife.

As soon as he tasted it, he said, 'Fine. I'll let you bake a cake for a client. But you do it at home. I'm not having an unqualified baker working in my bakery.'

I'd love to work her with Blake and with Sandra and the others, and I kind of assumed that *that* was gonna be my future. I guess not.

I look over at the door to the staff area, behind the counter.

'You going in?' he says, squeezing my arm again.

'I'm going in.'

He salutes me. 'Godspeed.'

*

When Superstar Frosting was set up, it started in Frank's kitchen at home. Inspired by a love of cakes, and — of course — a desire for even more fame, Frank soon moved out of his place and into professional kitchens on Sunset Boulevard, in the heart of the sunset strip. He wanted to be among all the night-life, all the stars, all the life of LA.

Sometimes I think about what Frank must have been like when he was young, when he was hungry for success. Because I don't see a dynamic, powerful man in front of me right now. I see a husk.

'So, you thought coming here on your day off might make me go easy on you?' he says.

He's sitting opposite me across a table, glaring at me.

'I'm so sorry, Frank. I had like, the worst day of my life.'

'You had the worst day of *your* life, huh? Well let me tell you, I didn't have such a good day, either.' Frank's white mustache twitches,

CHAPTER FIVE

and his dark blue eyes flare with anger. He's a big guy, with an imposing physique, but right now, it's his expression that's freaking me out. Pure malice. 'Do you know who Errol Bernstein is?'

I shake my head.

'He's the most powerful man in Hollywood. A producer. He makes and breaks careers every single day. Not just of actors and directors. Of everyone. Caterers. Make-up artists. Fuck, even fucking garbage collectors.' He's up now, pacing back and forth in the small office. 'That cake was for him, Harper. And when you didn't show, he went ballistic.'

My heart rate spikes, and then just stays there, fast and hard.

'Sorry.' My voice is quiet, submissive.

'Of course you're fucking sorry,' he says, shaking your head.

'I was in a traffic accident,' I blurt out. 'I had a fever. I didn't know whether I was coming or going.'

'So why didn't you call me?' he practically shouts. 'Why didn't you tell me that you were in trouble?'

'I'm scared,' I say, honestly. 'I didn't want you to shout at me. I was so excited to be making my first cake for you.'

He's shaking his head. 'I should have made you come here to bake it. I should have asked to see it first. It's my damn fault.'

'I'm sorry,' I say, again.

'I should fire you,' he says, his eyes burning bright, his hands on his hips. 'I should make it so that you can't get another job in a bakery in the whole damn state, never mind this city.'

I look down at my hands, twiddle my thumbs, try and take myself out of this moment. I wish I had Pudding right now, or any one of my stuffies. I need something, anything to stop me feeling so miserable. I should have told Frank.

LUCKY MOON

'You can fire me if you want,' I say. 'I deserve it.' Maybe I'll have to go back to my folks' home in Cheyenne, Wyoming. Probably have to work in my dad's auto-shop. Course I'll have to start living a lie again — hiding my Little stuff from Mom, pretending to be a fully-functional adult. I'll probably start to bump into people from high school. Probably end up getting bullied again.

No more baking dream. Back to reality.

I don't want to cry, don't want to show Frank how crappy I feel. But I can't help it. I feel the hot sting of tears on my cheek.

He breathes in deep. Pauses.

'If it wasn't for my new business, I would fire you.'

I look up at him, feeling the tiniest, most pathetic pang of hope.

'New business?'

'I'm getting into the... import business. I've got a big new client who want me to deliver cakes and baked goods from overseas.'

'Overseas?'

He nods. 'That's right. It's not glamorous, and there's no baking involved. I need a delivery girl. Someone to pick up goods from LAX and some other locations, and deliver them to clients across town. It's less pay.'

This seems so weird to me. All the while I worked as Frank's PA, I never got the impression that he had any interest in anything other than baking his own cakes and delivering them to high-profile clients. I don't get why he wants to be, basically, a courier.

Don't look a gift horse in the mouth, Harper.

'Sounds good,' I say, sniffing, trying to stop the tears from falling down my face.

He snorts. 'You don't need to lie to me, buttercup.'

There's a sudden waft of delicious aroma. Someone, somewhere in

CHAPTER FIVE

the bakery must have opened an oven. It's cinnamon, vanilla, and lots and lots of caramel. 'Fine,' I sniff. 'Sounds not good.'

'Take it or leave it.'

'I'll take it.'

'Good,' he says. 'You know, you're lucky you're such a sweet-looking little thing.'

My skin starts to crawl. Frank's mentioned my looks before. He's never overtly predatory, but he always makes me cringe with discomfort.

'My clients always like to see you,' he continues. 'Makes the cakes taste even better, they tell me.'

He's lying. I *hope* he's lying.

'So, is there any work for me today?' I ask, clasping my left elbow with my right hand.

'Not today. Why don't you go home. Rest. Make sure that you're over the sniffles. Then, when I need you, I'll call you.'

I cycle home with mixed emotions. I'm part devastated, part thankful, part grossed-out.

But if I knew the world I was about to get mixed up in, I wouldn't feel grateful. I would turn and cycle out of town, as fast as my wheels would carry me.

CHAPTER SIX

DANE

Smoke and whiskey. Oil and leather. Dim lights and hulking shapes.

It's good to be back in the Milk Shed.

'Pour me out a generous one, Roxy.'

The barmaid nods at me, her sleepy eyes gently smiling. 'Coming up, Boss.'

I don't normally drink, but today, I need something to calm my nerves. I glance up behind the bar. There's a bike up there, on full display for the discerning eyes of the clientele. It's a 1936 Harley-Davidson EL 'Knucklehead'. My favorite bike of all time.

To me, its simple lines and clean looks perfectly symbolize rugged, American freedom. It was the last bike that the Davidson brothers and William S. Harley designed together, and — even though I love modern Harleys — I miss the simplicity of those classic bikes.

Knuckleheads don't come for auction very often. It was a couple years ago that Bud gave me a call about the hog coming up for sale. He always seems to know whenever a vintage bike is coming onto the open market. I snapped it up.

'Penny for your thoughts?' Roxy places a tumbler of Irish Whiskey down on the bar. She puts her elbows down and cups her chin in her palms.

'They're not even worth a penny, babe.' Like most of the girls who work with DADDIES MC, Roxy's a Little. She's a good kid, but she's got problems. We took her in a couple years ago — she was on the run from another gang. Still gets trouble from time to time, but they're on the east coast. I think she feels safe here.

'I'm sure that's not true.'

'Just thinking about the club. The future. Motorbikes.'

'Typical Daddy,' she says, grinning.

I lift the tumbler to my lips and take a sip of the whiskey. It's harsh but good. As the burn fades, I'm left with sweetness, a smoky aroma, and the elusive, golden taste of honey.

Her eyes narrow. 'There's something else, isn't there?' she says. 'Something else on your mind?'

Other thing about Roxy is that she's so damn empathetic she's practically a fucking mind-reader.

I sigh. Now would be a great time to lie, Dane.

Nope. Can't do it.

'I met someone.'

Her eyes widen. 'As in, a girl?'

I nod.

'A Little?'

'I don't know. I think so, but when I asked her, she clammed up.'

Roxy nods, takes a glass, starts to polish it. 'She'll tell you in her own time. When you seeing her again?'

'That's the problem,' I say. 'I don't have her number. She doesn't have mine. And I don't know where she lives.'

'Jeez, Dane, you gotta get the contact details.'

'I dunno. It never came up.'

'Ugh, how frustrating! How long ago did you break up with Darlin'?'

I shake my head. 'Not long enough.'

Even thinking about Darlin' makes me wanna smash something. Can't believe I ever shared myself with her. She took me in, lied to me, then, when I broke it off with her for deceiving me, she went totally

CHAPTER SIX

berserk.

'I always knew she was bad news,' says Roxy. 'I mean, who smokes a dang pipe?'

I can't help but chuckle. At the time I'd been with Darlin', I'd found her old-timey tobacco pipe to be kinda cute. I'm not a smoker myself, but it hadn't bothered me. Now though, it stands out as a symptom of her ugly personality. Everything she did was about image, was about getting people to give her attention. There was nothing beneath the surface.

'Yeah, well, luckily I haven't seen or heard anything from her in quite a while.'

I feel a heavy hand on my shoulder. 'I always liked Darlin'. Thought that her craziness was a good counter to your mopey-ass intensity.'

It's Bud. I look round, and before I have a chance to take him in, he's giving me a bear hug. My face is all smushed up in the ribbed leather of his jacket. A moment later, I'm out of his embrace and left red-faced.

'Good to see you, Bud,' I grunt. 'Can I get you something to drink?'

'Whatever you're having.'

Roxy nods, pours him a measure of whiskey, pushes it across the bar.

'So where have you been? Cryin' about the result of the vote the other day?'

Bud is... a complicated character. How's the best way to put it? He's old-fashioned. In every respect. Kind of a biker dinosaur. He's rude. Crude. Very stuck in his ways and sure of his opinions. I can't actually think of the last time he changed his mind about anything.

And yet.

I love the guy. Can't help it. Cause Bud's about the closest thing to a

Dad that I have. I made some big mistakes when I was a kid. Damn near ruined my life. And Bud took me in, straightened me out, and taught me how to be a man.

'I'm not crying, Bud. But I am fucked off.'

He takes a swig of the whiskey, grimaces. 'This ain't bourbon, is it?'

His facial hair is getting ridiculous. He's always been a hairy guy, but recently, he's been going bushier and bushier. He's taking to braiding his beard at the front, and letting his sideboards grow to outrageous lengths. He's got emerald green eyes, and his hair is a shocking white color — with only a few stray darker hairs peppering the thick mass.

'It's Irish,' I admit. Bud's always been particular when it comes to liquor.

'Damn, Dane, shouldn't have this foreign crap in our club bar. Should be American, all the way.'

'We've got plenty of bourbon,' I say, sighing. 'Just like to have a little variety, too.'

The music cuts out, and a new track starts. Someone's put something into the jukebox. Hawk's standing there, still choosing. Then, the brutal first notes of Blood and Thunder by Mastodon sound out. Bud starts to tap his foot as Hawk walks over to us. He's wearing a leather vest and his huge arms are on full display. They're stitched with tattoos, and dirty with oil. He must have just come from work at the garage.

'Gentlemen,' he says, nodding at us.

'Hawk, settle a disagreement for us,' Bud says, gesturing to him as he walks over. 'When it comes to whiskey, is it bourbon, or Irish?'

'Pah!' Hawk says, pretending to spit. 'Far as I'm concerned, bourbon ain't even fucking whiskey. Made from corn. Whiskey should be from grain mash, far as I'm concerned.'

CHAPTER SIX

'Who let this fucking joker into the club?' Bud asks, looking round the bar for back-up.

'You did,' Hawk says, taking a seat next to us.

'Look,' I say, 'much as I love squabbling about drinks, that's not why I asked you two to meet me.'

'You already owe me a favor,' Hawk says, gesturing to Roxy. 'Fixed that bike up for you in double time. Had to bump a couple other projects for that. And that after you missed the vote, too.'

'I appreciate it,' I say. It's lucky that Hawk had space in his schedule to patch up Harper's bicycle.

'Was it a Harley?' Bud asks. He's a purist when it comes to bikes. You can't join DADDIES MC unless you own a Harley, and he doesn't really like the garage do any work on a bike that isn't a Harley, either. Seems dumb, I know, but he's fiercely loyal. I am too, but I'm a little more pragmatic when it comes to the clients we work with.

'Not exactly a Harley.' Hawk says, taking a sip from his own drink.

'Fucksake Hawk,' Bus says.

'Blame Dane. He's the one who's got me fixin' up some dame's bike.'

Bud chuckles. 'The pieces fall into place.'

I can see where this is going. Bud and Hawk teasing me for my inability to get Harper's number, or make any kind of move with her. I decide that I don't really feel like having that conversation right now.

'Look guys, let's focus on the matter in hand. Bud, you're the president of the club. Your word is law round here.'

Bud nods sagely. 'That *is* true.'

Insufferable. 'But look, I want to re-vote on the whole drug trafficking issue. It's too important.'

'If it was so important, how come you missed the damn vote?' Bud asks.

'I had something I needed to do.'

Bud scoffs. 'Son, you've always got something to do. And the funny thing is, you never tell us what it is you're up to.' This is a real trigger for Bud. How can I get through this minefield?

'I know I'm a private person, but that doesn't mean I'm not committed to the club.'

'You know Dane cares, Bud,' Hawk says, sticking up for me.

Bud grimaces. 'Look, we can't re-vote. Undermines the system too much. But no-one's stopping you from looking into this yourself.'

Huh. I hadn't really considered the idea of just going rogue and trying to break up the dealing myself.

'I'll help,' Hawk says, barely lifting an eyebrow.

'You will?'

'Sure. Got nothing better to do. Fixing engines all day gives me a hunger for some excitement.'

'You need to get yourself a Little,' Bud says, clapping Hawk on the back. 'Good-looking guy like you, should have no trouble. Not like poor old Shrek here.' He gestures to me. 'Why don't you just head down to The Nursery and pick out some tasty little thing. Find the right girl and you'll get yourself plenty of excitement.' He grins. 'Some trouble, most likely, too.'

'Thanks Bud,' I say. I'm not precious about my looks, but I know that I'm not handsome in the way that Hawk is. 'I happen to think I've got a rugged charm all of my own.

'Course you do. I'm sure one day, you'll find a nice female gorilla who'll love you for who you are.' He lets out a cruel, wheezing laugh.

'*That's* what you're looking for is it? Love?' I ask, pointedly.

'I don't have time for a relationship,' Hawk says. I can help but

CHAPTER SIX

notice the way his eyes flick to Roxy as he says those words.

'You know,' Bud says, suddenly serious. 'If you *do* want to look into the drug smuggling, I can give you some info.'

This guy is the most connected biker in LA. It's not just bikes coming up for sale that he knows all about.

'Go on,' I say, playing with my glass.

'A little birdie told me that the Blood Fuckers are in on this.'

Ugh. Not only is it a rival MC, it's the craziest, most reckless club in town. The Blood Fuckers are the kind of club that gives bikers a bad name. They act like a mafia, simple as that, hustling drugs and so much worse across the city. I'm not put off by the fact that I'm gonna go up against the BF, but it's definitely daunting.

'Damn,' Hawk says. 'You're gonna *need* my help.'

'I've got something else for you. An old friend of mine told me that there's a deal going down in a couple days. There's a deal going down at the port. I'll send you the details. Go check it out, if you want.'

'Fuck,' Hawk hisses.

'Just go in slow, quiet,' Bud says. 'You don't want the foot-soldiers. You want the head-honcho. Satan himself.'

It's not just a nick-name. The head of the Blood Fuckers literally calls himself Satan. No-one knows his identity. Mother-fucker's like a comic-book villain.

'Be good to finally uncover that asshole.'

He drains his glass.

'Bud,' I say, 'how do you know all this shit?'

He stands, winks. 'Ask me no questions, and I'll tell you no lies.' Then he turns and walks out the bar, stopping to admire the posterior of a girl bent over the pool table. He looks back at us, and mimes spanking the girl's ass. I shake my head at him, eyes burning seriously.

'Lighten up,' he mouths, before walking out of the bar.

'Guy's a fucking liability,' I say to Hawk.

'Whatever,' Hawk says. 'I want to know all about this girl, Dane. I'm gonna buy you another drink, then you're gonna fucking spill the beans, biker-boy.'

I can't help but grin.

'You damn gossip,' I say.

'You better bet your ass I'm a gossip. Now get ready to fill me in on all the dirty details.'

As he orders a drink, I wish I had dirtier details to share.

CHAPTER SEVEN

HARPER

'So come on,' Felicity leans across the table and stirs a spoonful of brown sugar into her flat-white, 'what was it like to be in an outlaw biker's apartment?'

'I don't think he was an outlaw!'

Felicity looks under the table, pulls up a bright green backpack, then grabs a pad of paper from inside.

'Are you taking notes?'

She nods. 'You bet. I'm working on a screenplay based on a biker gang right now. I wanna make sure that it's as authentic as possible.'

Felicity works as an assistant at Galactic, one of the biggest movie studios in town. Her dream is to work as a script writer, and she's always got some idea on the go. But if I know Felicity and her crazy imagination, there will be more to this biker story than meets the eye.

'Haven't biker dramas been done to death by now, Flick?' I ask, using my pet name for her.

She grins. 'Not the way I'm gonna write it.'

'Oh?'

'OK. So. Think Bikers. And shape-shifting aliens. With a dash of vampirism. And a little pinch of pro-wrestling thrown in.'

I burst out laughing. I can never tell whether Flick is joking or not.

'Don't laugh!' she says, looking faux-scandalized. 'This is a very serious project!'

'I can see why you need to get the biker parts as authentic as possible,' I say, smiling.

'Exactly!'

It feels so good to be relaxing with Felicity. We're in Caffiends, a new coffee bar just of Sunset. It kinda feels more like a laboratory then a café. The bar is a solid white slab of marble, with strange coffee machines built into it. None of them look like a filter machine, or even a classic espresso thingy. There's a variety of weird-looking flasks and mugs at one end of the bar. I'm still waiting for my coffee — a Peruvian pour-over. Every now and then, I glance over at the guy who's preparing it — a lean, scientist-looking dude — as he pours water over a filter so slow that he looks like he's in slow-motion.

This place isn't really my scene, but Flick loves it.

'Well,' I say, 'he was very... gruff.'

She starts to scribble in her notebook.

'And kinda mean-seeming. He had all this freaky stuff on the walls. Heavy-metal posters and even antlers. Everything was dark. Like his walls were black!'

'Sounds scary!' gasps Felicity, looking up at me with her big blue eyes.

'It was. But I always felt really safe, too. I mean, I coulda been in a serial-killer's dungeon for all I knew. He made me feel at home. Even got a doctor to come check me out, make sure that I wasn't hurt or anything.'

She's still writing. Without looking up, she says, 'And, how hot was he?' She tries to sound innocent, but I know exactly what she's getting it.

'Interesting question,' I say. 'Doesn't seem exactly relevant for making a TV show authentic.

She pauses, looks up at me. 'It's crucial I know precisely how attractive my characters are, Harper. You wouldn't understand, it's a screen-writer thing.' She gives me a haughty snort. She's just fooling

CHAPTER SEVEN

around, but she's damn good at it.

'Well,' I say, 'in that case... he was smoking hot! Like, not conventionally attractive maybe. And he had this big scar down his face. Big black beard. But there was something about him. He was so confident, so sure of himself. And his body... oh my god.'

'Totally... ripped... bod...' she says, smiling, writing the words down in big letters on her sheet. 'Got it.'

Then, she draws a little heart on the page, and writes, '*Harper Loves Dane*' inside it.

'I do not!' I gasp, punching her arm.

'So, when are you seeing him again?' she asks.

I feel it again, the shame of my identity, in the pit of my stomach like a rock. 'Never,' I sigh.

She looks confused. 'Harper, this isn't how this story ends. He saved you. Nursed you back to health. Fixed your bike. And you're not gonna see him again.'

'We're not compatible,' I say. I'm so bad at lying, and Flick knows it. But she also knows not to push it.

'Fair enough,' she says. 'Well, me and Marty are over.'

Marty is this ultra-rich producer that Felicity has been dating on and off for a couple months. I never really liked him, always thought he was a bit... fake?

'What happened?'

'He called me Janet.' She leans in and whispers the next words. 'In bed.'

'Oh no! I didn't think stuff like that actually happened in real life.'

'I didn't think getting saved by super-hot bikers actually happened in real life.' She shrugs. 'Turns out, Janet is his wife.'

'Oh no!' I cover my mouth with my hand. 'That's so shitty!' For some reason, as I cuss, I think about Dane, giving me a disappointed look and threatening me with punishment. The thought of it sends a little pulse of excitement through me.

'I'm back on the market,' she says. 'So, if you meet any other bikers, point them my way.'

I think about mentioning Ripper, but he's *definitely* too old for Felicity. Plus — I don't even know if he's single. Probably not.

'Will do,' I say. Poor Flick. Working hard in the hope that she gets promoted. Trying to make connections to give her a foot in the door of the movie industry. I feel for her.

She takes another sip of her drink, then swirls it absentmindedly around. 'I'm gonna have finished my coffee before yours even gets here. So what's going on with your job?'

'Things are kinda... weird.'

'What's weird in the world of baking?'

'I'm not really a baker any more. I'm more like a courier now. Frank's got me cycling round LA, picking up cakes and delivering them to clients.'

'Doesn't sound *too* weird.'

'Right. Except these clients are not your typical cake orderers.'

She laughs. 'Who's your typical cake orderer?'

'Oh, you know. A mom who's too busy to make a cake for her kid's birthday. Or a boss who wants to impress a worker. These people are like... I dunno. Tough.'

'Tough?'

'Yeah like, if I didn't know better, I'd think they were gangsters or something.'

Now she's laughing her head off. 'So, you're scooting around Hollywood, delivering illicit cakes to shady gangsters? Maybe they're

CHAPTER SEVEN

planning on giving their enemies diabetes to slowly kill them!' She snorts out a laugh. 'Or maybe the frosting's laced with arsenic. Hey, that's a good idea for a script!'

'Don't turn my life story into entertainment!' I say, as Felicity keeps laughing.

'Madam, your Peruvian pour over?' The whip-thin barista has finally brought my coffee over to me. It's in a tiny metal cup, presented to me on a tray silver tray. There's a little tub of something that looks like dirty salt next to the cup.

'What's that?' I ask, as he lays the tray down on our table.

'Smoked salt,' he replies. 'Smell it before each mouthful.'

'I love this place,' Felicity says, grinning.

When the barista leaves, I lift the tiny bowl of smoked salt to my nose, inhaling deeply. Instantly, I start to hack and cough. 'Ack! Cripes! Smells of cigarettes! What the-?'

Felicity starts to laugh. 'You remind me so much of a little kid sometimes, Harper. You're so damn cute! Can't remember the last time I heard someone say cripes.'

I want to come out to Felicity so badly. I'm sure she'd accept me as a Little. I just can't bring myself to.

'Thanks, I think,' I say, finally lifting the cup of coffee to my mouth. It smells so good. 'I hope this is worth the wait.'

Just as I'm about to taste the dark brown brew, my phone chirps with a notification. Damn it. It's Frank.

I need you to pick up a delivery from LAX and I need it done two hours ago. Get there now or there'll be trouble.

My coffee sits on the table, taunting me.

'You've got time to drink it, right?' Felicity's voice is warm, soft, supportive.

I shake my head. 'Not if I want to live to drink coffee ever again,' I say.

Flick passes me my bright pink helmet, and I plonk it on my head. 'Feel free to drink my coffee,' I say. 'Just go easy on the smoked salt.'

She grins. 'I swear, Harper, you're just about the sweetest girl I know. Be careful on the roads.'

I nod.

*

Cycling as fast as my legs can carry me, it still takes me over an hour to get to the airport. The sun's beating down, and by the time I reach the ping Frank sent me I feel dehydrated. Dane would be telling me off right now, passing me cup after cup after water.

Sometimes I think about those strong, rugged fingers passing me a little sippy-cup to drink from. I think about him looking at me tenderly as I say, 'Thank you, Daddy.'

It's just a dream though. I ruined whatever chances I had with Dane when I clammed up. Typical me.

It's weird, the ping isn't for an arrivals lounge. It isn't even inside the main airport.

I find myself cycling down a back alley, behind one of the terminals, and eventually, I reach a dead-end. It smells round here of garbage and fuel, a dirty, rubbery scent that makes me feel deeply uncomfortable.

Someone's waiting for me. He's tall, and slim, wearing a white sleeveless shirt and torn, faded jeans. He does not look like a baker. His hair is long and slick, tied into a ponytail at the back.

When he sees me, he takes the cigar from his mouth and throws it down the ground before screwing it into the ground with a heel.

CHAPTER SEVEN

'You're late, Chica,' he says, with a heavy accent.

'Sorry,' I say, pulling off my helmet. My hair's all sweaty underneath.

'S'OK baby, I forgive you.' He gives me a nasty little smile.

'So, what's so special about these cakes?' I ask.

He passes over a tower of three cake boxes to me. They're tied together with pink silk ribbon.

The guy looks at me for a second, clearly confused. Then, as though remembering something, he says, 'Oh right — the cakes. Uh, I dunno, they've got like, sparkles on them.'

'Sparkles you can't get in this country.'

'Right, right.' He nods, takes another short, thin cigar from a tin in his pocket. 'Special sparkles. So, you single, baby?' He lights the cigar and grins, showing off a mouthful of gleaming gold teeth.

'Um, no,' I lie, anxiously grabbing my arm.

'Damn. Boyfriend's a lucky man.' He blows a cloud of smoke out in front of him.

'Have you been smoking near the cakes?' I ask.

'Yeah. Why?'

Because the smoke will ruin the flavor, that's why. I don't say that, though. 'No, doesn't matter, just interested is all.'

'Anyway, I gotta run, sugar. Hopefully I'll see you again though. I'd like to see a *whole lot* more of you, if you know what I mean.'

I think the safest option is to not say a word. So I stay silent. It throws him a bit, and after a moment, he just shrugs, then leaves.

My heart's pounding until he's well out of sight. This all feels so wrong. Why is Frank doing this?

Suddenly, I get a terrible feeling. My heart rate spikes again, and I decide that I need to check something, just to be sure.

LUCKY MOON

I undo the pink ribbon, and carefully open the top of the three boxes.

It's cake. Thank god. Hardly decorated — just a thick layer of white buttercream, but cake nonetheless. Obviously, there's no sparkles.

Just then, I get a message from Frank.

Heard you picked up the cakes. Well done. Here's where you're taking them.

It's another ping. This time, it's somewhere in the port. Even though my brain's screaming at me to just leave the cakes here and cycle away somewhere, far away, I load them up onto the front of my bike, then I start to pedal.

CHAPTER EIGHT

DANE

'You think they'll be able to see us from up here?'

Hawk's lying down next to me, binoculars pressed to his eyes.

'No reason for them to be looking up,' I reply. 'Unless we give them a reason to. Like, you know, sunlight reflected in a pair of fucking pointless binocs.'

Hawk grins, lowers them. 'Can't do covert ops without binoculars, bud. Trust me, I'm ex-military.'

'Really? You were in the military?' I'm being sarcastic, of course. Hawk never damn shuts up about his time in the army. 'Fuck man, thanks for your service.'

'Get fucked, needle dick,' Hawk says, grinning a shit-eating grin.

'You military types, always fixated on dick size,' I say.

'Whatever,' he says. 'You know, when I agreed to help you, I didn't think we'd just be hanging out on a damn roof all day long, waiting for something to happen.'

'Yeah,' I grunt. 'Good of Bud to give us the place and the day, just a shame that he didn't give us the exact time this thing is due to go down.'

We're in the port, away from the main commercial docks and the pleasure boating. Don't really come to the San Pedro district much, and honestly, I kinda wonder how a drug deal going down in this part of town is actually connected to our patch in the Fashion District.

Obviously, a bunch of clothes come into the port from China on massive container ships. But that's not normally the way that drugs come into the country. Normally, contraband comes in over the border, or at the airport, smuggled in someone's cargo.

LUCKY MOON

Still, Bud's intel's normally rock solid. I trust the old dude without question. So here we are, on a rooftop in San Pedro, waiting for something to happen.

I've been waiting even longer than a day though. Since Bud told me about the deal, I feel like I've not been able to think about anything but what's about to go down.

Been so wound up I even worked a damn shift at the Milk Shed. Anything to try to take my mind off this deal. Sometimes I worry that I care too much about drugs, that I shouldn't worry about things that aren't my problem. Maybe Bud's right.

Then I think about what happened to my parents. What happened to me. And that righteous fire gets lit again inside me. This is where I'm meant to be. This is what I'm meant to be doing.

'So, what's the plan?' Hawk says. 'When the deal goes down?' He lifts up his shirt, shows me that he's packing heat.

'Hawk, you dumbass, what did you bring that for?'

'Protection, of course. What do you think? Not gonna be using it as a damn paperweight, that's for sure.'

'You know by bringing that thing, you've increased the chances of us getting into a firefight by about a million percent?'

'Whatever,' he says.

'You say that a lot,' I say. 'Always tryna' pretend you don't give a shit about anyone, huh? But I know you care.'

'Hey, we got movement.' Hawk points down, lifts his binoculars. Hard not to feel like he's getting a real childish kick out of this, like he's playing cops and robbers with a big brother. I wonder whether, in this scenario, we're the cops or robbers.

I look down, and see a young mother pushing a pram in front of her.

CHAPTER EIGHT

'You think she's moving the drugs to the Blood Fuckers? Or you think maybe the BF are letting new moms join their super hardcore motorbike gang?'

'You can never tell,' Hawk starts.

'Maybe the kid's the smuggler,' I say. 'Maybe he's the criminal mastermind behind the wave of ODs and new addicts in the fashion district.'

We both watch as the pair walk straight past the warehouse we're watching. Hawk sighs. 'Maybe Bud got his info wrong this time. How long we been here?'

'Four hours.'

'Four fucking hours I coulda been making some money at the shop.'

'You knew what you were letting yourself in for when you agreed to help,' I say.

'Yeah, well, I'm getting a little tired. I was up late last night.'

'Talking to Roxy?' I ask, giving him a sly wink.

'I'm not into Roxy,' he says.

'Sure. Course you're not. You just look at her that way cause you've got a lazy eye.'

He shakes his head. 'Look, I'm not the one who's willing to sacrifice his morals and ethics just cause a pretty girl bats her eyelashes at me.'

'She was in danger, Hawk. I'm a member of Daddies MC. The whole point of the club is to care for those in need, isn't it?'

'I guess so.' He agrees. 'Right now, I'm the one in need. Of a sleep. You mind keeping watch for me while I catch forty winks.'

Anger flashes up inside me briefly, then it dies away. Hawk and me have got too much history for me to bust his ass too badly over stuff like this. I'm grateful to him for coming and helping at all.

'Sure,' I say. 'You get your beauty sleep, and I'll do all the work.'

LUCKY MOON

'Perfect,' he says, grinning. 'Life's natural order's been restored.' He rolls over, pulls a hat over his eyes, and within minutes, he's sleeping like a baby.

I grab his binoculars and settle in. This is gonna be a long day.

*

There are a couple more false alarms. An older lady with a shopping cart. A pair of young lovers, practically chewing each other's faces off.

Finally, I see a gang of what look to be thugs. They look shifty as fuck. Four of them, walking with a street limp, laughing and joking together.

I give Hawk a shove, and he comes to.

'Roxy?' he says, not even awake yet.

'You're a fucking disgrace, Hawk Anders. If you tell me one more time that you're not into Roxy, I swear I'm gonna go insane.'

Takes him a moment to realize what's going on, then he shakes his head.

'Just a dream, man. Doesn't mean anything. Why d'you wake me?'

'Eyes on the street,' I say. 'Got some gangbangers coming in hot.'

He turns over, looks over the edge of the roof, straight down at the gang.

'We're in business,' he says. Then, moments later, the four young men walk straight past the building.

'False alarm,' I say.

'You think?' Hawk says.

'Sorry brother,' I say. 'Get back to sleeping if you want. I'll keep my eyes open.'

'Nah, I'm up now. Hey — you think that could be our target?'

CHAPTER EIGHT

I can hear the joke in his voice, but I follow his eyes anyway. And when I see what he's looking at, my breath catches in my chest.

'Hang on,' he continues. 'Don't I know that bike?'

Holy fuck. It's Harper. She's cycling her brand new bike right up to the front door of the warehouse we're watching.

'What the fuck?' I whisper under my breath. Hawk looks at me. He's no idiot. He knows exactly what's going on here.

'That's the girl? From the other day? The girl who you said definitely *wasn't* on drugs when you knocked her off her bike?'

'That's her,' I say, shaking my head. 'Maybe she's gonna go p-'

She doesn't. She pulls up to a railing next to the warehouse entrance, then chains her bike up. She's wearing her pink helmet again, and today, she's got on a cute little outfit — all frills, wrapped up in a dungaree dress that's so damn cute it's making me feel all funny.

Huh. Until I met Harper, I didn't even think that 'cute' was a quality I looked for in a girl. Guess you learn something new every day.

'She tricked you pretty fucking good.' Hawk says. He grabs the binoculars and looks through. 'Damn, Dane, you weren't kidding when you said she was hot. Whoo-hoo she's delightful. You've got no chance with someone like her, Amigo.'

'Alright,' I say, snatching the binocs from him and holding them up to my eyes. 'Enough ogling.'

'Thought you said you weren't interested.'

'When did I say that, bonehead?'

Harper unstraps a tower of three boxes from the front of her bicycle. What are you doing, Harper? I mean, is it possible that this is all some dumb misunderstanding? Is she just delivering cakes to a warehouse worker?

'Maybe I misheard.'

LUCKY MOON

I watch as Harper takes her bright pink helmet off, slings it over her seat. I love that hair — so fiery and dark at the same time — like rich, dark maple.

'If she was on drugs, it wasn't just me she tricked. Ripper fell for the act, too. Maybe I'm being naive, but I just can't believe that Harper's a fucking drug smuggler.'

Harper walks up to the front door, trying to balance the stack of cake boxes in one hand as she presses the buzzer. She says something, then steps back, before adjusting her hair.

As she waits, I find myself starting to panic. That insane protective streak that woke in me a couple days ago flares up. I'm too far away from her. If something crazy happens, if someone comes out and hurts her, then I can't get down in time to guard her.

I don't have much time to worry about her though, because after just ten seconds or so, the roller door starts to shift up. I watch as it slowly lifts, revealing a pair of female legs. Whoever she's meeting has bare legs, and a pair of extremely tight hot pants.

A moment later, I see a ripped leather jacket.

When I see her face, my mouth falls open. I literally can't believe what I'm seeing. It's worse than a ghost. It's like I'm seeing a monster — a scene from a horror film playing out in front of my eyes. I'm powerless to stop it.

Because Harper isn't just meeting a Blood Fucker. She's meeting Darlin'. My ex. The woman who made my life hell. She's wearing Blood Fucker colors, and she's smiling evilly at Harper.

'Is that-' Hawk starts, before I hold up my hand to silence him.

'Not. A. Fucking. Word.' I hiss.

Harper — clearly awkward — hands over the stack of cake boxes to Darlin', who smiles and rests a hand on Harper's arm. This whole thing

CHAPTER EIGHT

is so weird — I can barely believe it's happening.

'What are we gonna do?' Hawk says, keeping his voice low.

'Don't worry,' I reply. 'I'm all over this.'

CHAPTER NINE

HARPER

What. A. Day.

I don't think I've ever been so happy to see the run-down facade of my apartment block. That was honestly one of the weirdest experiences of my life.

The woman at the docks, who took the stack of cakes from me, was one of the most unpleasant people I've ever met. She kept calling me a 'little baker bitch' and laughing. She stank of weed, and when she leaned in close, I smelled booze on her breath, too.

I'm still terrified. Still shaking.

I hop off old reliable, and chain her up, before heading up the stairs to my place. I know I'm just being paranoid, but I can't shake the feeling that someone's watching me. Sends a shiver running up and down my spine.

I need something to calm me down, and luckily enough, I know that it's waiting for me in my apartment. A nice big mug of hot chocolate with so many marshmallows stuffed into the mug that it's basically impossible to drink.

I want to get lost in a TV show. Or maybe a book! I really like to read — I started the Witcher books recently (I'm a massive fantasy nerd). That's what I'll do. I'll drink a nice warm drink and get lost in the world of Geralt and Triss.

I slip my key into my door and turn the handle.

But when I open the up, all my plans for the evening get flushed down the drain.

'Well, well, well, you're back.' That southern twang. That big fat face. Those aviators. It's the biker from the other day, and he's sitting in my armchair, looking straight at me.

'What are you doing in my apartment?'

'Just thought I'd drop by. You asked to see my credentials the other day. So I brought them round.' He stands up to his full, imposing height, and shoots his hand behind him. When he reveals it again, he's holding a big, curved knife.

'Oh my god,' I say, the words mumbling and tumbling out of me. No-one's ever pulled a knife on me before. I feel my legs go weak beneath me, my heart start to pound in my chest.

My heart. The thing he's gonna plunge that knife into me if I don't do what he says.

'Come here sweetheart,' he says.

I should turn, should run, should never come back to the place.

But I can't. When someone tells me what to do, I do what they say. It's like I'm powerless in the face of authority. Even if that authority is just a big damn knife.

I step inside the apartment. The thug steps toward me. Fear grips me.

Then, another voice.

'You drop that fucking toothpick and get the fuck outta here before I rearrange your face so bad your mommy can't recognize you.'

I look back over my shoulder, and see Dane standing behind me. I feel a sudden rush of hope, of relief, but when I see that he's not armed, the fear starts to creep back.

'Dane O'Fucking Brien,' says the man with the knife. 'Fancy seeing you here.' He tosses the knife from hand to hand. 'You still run with those perverts and assholes in Daddies MC?'

Dane steps in, putting himself between me and the other guy.

CHAPTER NINE

'Baby, kicking you out of the club was the best decision I ever made.'

Wait, the six-foot four guy the size of a freaking country is called *Baby*? Even though I'm more anxious than I can just about ever remember, I feel this sudden, insane desire to laugh. Thankfully, I manage to control myself.

'Best thing to ever happen to me,' Baby replies. 'Got myself a new crew now. Much more inclusive. And I'm actually making some cash now.'

'Is this how you're making your money? Putting the squeeze on innocent young women who just happen to be living in the wrong neighborhood?'

'Not *just* that, but, you know, it's a living.'

Dane shakes his head. 'Enough small talk. Get the fuck out of here. No ifs, no buts.'

Baby puts a finger on the tip of his knife. 'No can do, brother. I'm here to get my money. And this little cutie owes two hundred bucks.'

'Hey, the other day it was a hundred and fifty!' I can't help but butt in.

'Yeah well, interest is a bitch, isn't it?'

'I'll tell you one more time, Baby,' Dane says, ignoring my intrusion, 'you get the fuck outta here right now, or you'll regret it.'

Baby considers his options. 'Fine,' he sighs. 'I'm going.'

There's something about the way he says that though, that gets my nerves up. And as he starts walking towards the door with his knife still in his hand, I can almost feel the tension start to rise. Dane must feel it too, because he shifts from side to side.

The moment that Baby is within striking distance, Dane tenses up. And when Baby's attack comes, he's totally ready.

Baby jabs forward, aiming straight for Dane's chest. But as he moves, Dane quickly dodges to the side. He swoops down, ducking low, and then pummels Baby once — twice — with his massive, powerful fists. The blows are so hard, so monstrous, that I can almost feel them. Baby lets out two huge cries of pain, and then, before he has a chance to respond to the attack, Dane pounds him again, in the hand this time. The knife flies loose, spinning across the room.

I shriek with fear, jumping backward. Even though I'm nowhere near the path of the spinning blade, I imagine it hitting me, sinking into my body. I feel like I'm gonna pass out.

'You stupid fuck,' Dane shouts. He shapes up to hit Baby again, but before he has a chance, Baby makes a break for it, loping out of the door, heading out into the evening light.

I look over at Dane, marveling at his bravery. I look his incredible physique up and down. It's at this moment, right now, that I know I want this man. I want him to protect me. I want him to nurture me.

Fuck. I want him to be my Daddy.

'Dane!' I cry out. 'You saved me.'

He turns and looks at me, his eyes burning with intensity. 'I'm not here to save you, Harper. I'm here to find out what the fuck is going on in my turf.'

*

'So, run this past me again, because I'm still having trouble taking it all in.'

'OK,' I say. 'I'll do my best.'

We're sitting in my kitchen, across the table from each other. Dane's definitely calmed down a lot since he first came in, but I still feel like

CHAPTER NINE

he's trying to catch me out.

'So, you were just delivering *cakes* to that warehouse in San Pedro?' I can't take my eyes off his intense face. There's so much I want to ask him. About how he got that scar. About how he found my place. About how he knows Baby.

But I can't.

Instead, I just nod. 'I work for a company called Superstar Frosting. We bake and deliver cakes to celebrities in th-'

'You think that woman you delivered your cakes to was a celebrity?'

'Well,' I say, indignant, 'I mean. No. She's not one of our usual clients.'

He pauses for a moment, narrows his eyes. For a moment, I feel like he's looking straight into me, deep into my soul.

'You're telling me the truth, aren't you?'

'Dane, you've got to believe me — I don't know what's going on. Ever since Frank — my boss — demoted me, all I've been doing is just running these weird, un-decorated cakes across town. From LAX to the docks. From Beverly Hills to the Fashion District.'

His eyes widen. 'Fuck, Harper. They're using you as a mule. That's why you have to move these cakes all over the place.'

'It's not drugs,' I say. 'I checked. It's just cakes in those boxes.'

'Yeah,' he says. 'But what's *inside* the cakes?'

Oh my god. This whole week, I've been smuggling drugs. I've been breaking the lay. I've been in danger, this whole time, and I had no idea.

'You alright?' Dane asks. 'You've gone really fucking white.'

'I think so,' I say, but my head's swimming. White motes flash before my eyes. 'Just having some trouble taking this all in.'

'That's my line,' Dane says.

'So, who have I been delivering the cak- *the drugs* to? Who have I been getting them from?'

He gives me a serious look. 'Well, I actually happen to know the woman you met today. She's bad news. A psycho, really. She's always been a criminal, and I know that she's got a violent history.' He pauses for a second, as if trying to work out whether to tell me something. Then, he says, 'Actually, you're not gonna believe this, but she's my fucking ex.'

I'm stunned. 'Your ex? As in. Ex-girlfriend?'

'Yeah.' He looks embarrassed. Ashamed. 'I kinda like bad girls, I guess.'

He doesn't know it, but he just slapped me in the face.

'Bad girls, huh?' Well, any chance I had of anything happening with Dane just went up in smoke.

'Well, yeah,' he says. 'Only type of woman I've ever been with, anyway. But like, I haven't been with lots of women. I just mean. Ugh.'

'It's OK, I get it.' I say. I don't quite know what's happening between us. But there's something here. Something weird. But something. I let out a long sigh. 'You know, this evening, all I wanted to do was to have a hot chocolate and relax.'

'Yeah? I could make you a hot chocolate. If you like.'

It's a surprise. The first truly nice one of the day. 'OK,' I say, feeling slightly bashful. 'That would be lovely.'

'Obviously, I don't know how my hot chocolate making skills will stack up against the expectations of a professional baker.'

'If it's warm and sweet, I'll drink it,' I say. As Dane gets up and heads for the stove, I realize I do feel a little bit better. Just knowing that he's on my side.

It doesn't take long for Dane to whip up a drink for me. He works silently, and is really focused. He blends the cocoa powder with sugar

CHAPTER NINE

and a splash of milk, making a paste, then he pours in hot milk, stirring furiously, until a frothy, steamy mug is ready.

'Mmmmm,' I say, taking a sip, letting the silky-smooth drink coat my tongue. 'That's delicious!'

'Glad you think so,' he says, taking a seat next to me. 'Look, Harper, I've been thinking.'

'While you made the hot chocolate?'

He grins, nods. 'Pretty much. I'm a quick thinker. Tend to be a bit impulsive, I guess. Anyway. Here's what I've decided.'

Decided?

'I'm gonna look after you.' He crosses his huge arms across his chest. 'Until this whole situation is sorted. You're an innocent young woman. I'm not gonna let you get hurt.'

My mouth hangs open. I'm stunned.

'Hey,' he says, his voice soft, 'you've got a chocolate mustache going on. Just so you know.'

'Oh,' I say, gawping like a fish. I wipe the back of my hand across my mouth.

'I'm serious. I'm not going to leave your side. I'm gonna make sure that no-one — not your boss, not these thugs, not the drug dealers — harms a single hair on your head. You're involved with some serious shit, through no fault of your own. I hate the thought of you dealing with it alone. I'm not gonna let that happen. So, what do you say? Can I stay?'

'Do I have a choice?' It's a bratty thing to say, but it's the first thing that pops into my head.

'Course you do. You can tell me to get out, to leave you alone, and I'll never bother you again. But I wouldn't recommend it.'

He's offering to be some kind of bodyguard? To watch over me like a guardian angel?

'So, you'll sleep here?'

He nods. 'I want you to know that I'm a man of honor, Harper. And I believe in a certain code of conduct when it comes to women. I asked the other day if you are a Little. You don't have to talk about it, but I want to explain why. My motorbike club, Daddies MC, is all about protecting vulnerable women. The other bikers in the club are Daddy Doms.'

'And you're not?' The question leaves me lips so fast I don't consider the ramifications.

'Well, I don't really know. I'm hoping to find that all out. Still working out who I am.'

So he *might* be a Daddy Dom. I'm suddenly imagining what it might be like to be with him. To feel him near me.

Then he looks me in the eye. 'But what I do know is, if you're looking for someone to look after you like a Daddy would — I'm your guy. I won't let you down.'

I believe him. Taking another sip of my drink, I try to get my head around what's going on here. I should make a list of pros and cons, try to measure up all the varia-

No. I'm gonna do what Dane does. Make an impulsive decision.

'OK.' I say. 'I want your help.'

'Good,' he says. 'And I want to ask you one more thing. Something you can definitely say no to. Thing is, I feel like you and I *have* something. I don't know what it is, but I've just got this feeling that I could find out about myself with you. Is that something you'd like to explore?'

As he's talking, I feel my heart pounding in my chest. There's only one answer I can give. 'I'd like that,' I say, my voice quiet and meek.

CHAPTER NINE

His expression changes, becomes surprised and soft. 'Well,' he says, slightly hoarse, 'we'll talk about that more tomorrow. I guess.'

'I guess.'

CHAPTER TEN

DANE

Sleeping on the floor again. Seems like this is starting to become something of a habit for me.

I barely slept last night. I was listening out for small sounds, anything which could be Baby coming to finish what he started. The fact the he knows where Harper lives is definitely a problem. I might have to relocate us. Hopefully, Harper won't have a problem with that.

When I wasn't listening out for sounds, I was messaging Hawk. Even though she hasn't said it in so many words, I'm convinced that Harper's a Little. She's a natural sub, always following instructions, and I feel as though I can just sense her trying to open up and enter Little Space whenever she's near me. I spoke to Hawk for hours, picking his brain about how to help Harper relax, and how to bring out the Little in her. He's got *lots* of experience with Littles, and I badly need access to that experience.

Even though Hawk's my best friend, he can be kinda annoying sometimes. But last night, he was fantastic. He didn't tease me, he didn't troll me. He just gave me simple information as and when I asked for it. So this morning, I feel like I've got a fighting chance of getting to know Harper — the real Harper.

And by getting to know the real Harper, maybe I'll get to know the real me.

Suddenly, my thoughts are interrupted.

'Are you awake?' Harper's voice is muffled by her pillow.

'Mmmhmm,' I grunt back.

'Kinda feels like we're having a sleepover.'

'Sure does,' I reply.

'Sorry I went to sleep so quick last night,' she says. I look up, and see that she's crawled to the edge of her bed. She's looking down at me.

Damn. She looks amazing. Those sleepy eyes and that bed-head hair. I could just eat her up.

'What you sorry about that for?'

'Well when I was a girl, and I'd have sleepovers, my friend and I would stay up really late, chatting and joking. It was kinda like a tradition. Coulda done that last night, I guess.'

'Sounds fun. Maybe we can do that another night?'

'Yeah. I'd like that.'

'I was thinking we go grab some breakfast together. I've had some ideas that I'd like to run past you — make sure that we're on the same wavelength.'

'That sounds nice, let's go!' She jumps out of bed and starts doing what look like star jumps, but way cuter.

'What you doing?' I ask, smiling.

'Getting pumped up. Feels like a big important day. After yesterday, I kinda feel lucky to be alive.' She fixes me with a goofy grin. 'Anything seems possible.' Her eyes widen. 'Oooo do I get to ride on your bike again? Please?'

'That could be arranged. But first, before we do anything else, you're gonna need to have a shower.'

She looks at me like I've gone mad. 'A shower? Ugh. Boring!'

'It may be boring young lady, but no-one rides Angeline without having a clean butt.'

'Who's Angeline?'

'My bike, of course.'

She giggles. 'Your bike's got a name?'

CHAPTER TEN

'Sure,' I say. 'It'd feel a little weird if she didn't. To me at least.'

'And she's a girl?'

'Of course. I wouldn't ride a guy. Not really my style.'

She whistles a cute little wolf whistle. 'Sexy.'

I grunt out a laugh. 'You'll have to tell her that.'

'Hey,' she says, 'I just realized something. Angeline is like your stuffie.'

Ah, stuffies. Hawk was talking about them last night. Littles often have a special relationship with their soft toys.

'I've never thought about it like that,' I say. 'But I guess you're right, in a way. Of course, I'd never snuggle up with Angeline in bed. She's a little bit bulky — although don't tell her I told that.'

She laughs, rolls over in bed so that her head dangles over the edge and she's looking at me upside-down.

'Do you have a stuffie, up-side-down girl?'

'I do,' she says. 'A little cupcake, called pudding.'

'What is it about baking?' I ask. 'Seems like it's all you ever think about.'

'Have you *tried* cake?' she says, rolling around again.

'A couple times.'

'Not good cake, clearly, otherwise you wouldn't be asking me what I like about baking.'

'I guess you'll have to bake a good cake for me.'

'Hmmm,' she says, resting her chin in her palms. 'I think you should bake for me. Might help you to discover yourself. I can see you wearing an apron. Covered in flour and sugar. And I bet with those big hands, you'd be an expert with a piping bag in no time.'

I can *feel* her relaxing, feel her personality start to come out. It's amazing, the best feeling in the world.

'A piping bag, eh? Sounds a bit fruity.'

'Yeah. You squeeze it. Firm pressure. Apply it evenly with both hands. Grip it confidently wi-.'

'And you're definitely talking about a piping bag, huh?' I say, smiling.

'You know, for an aspiring Daddy, you can be quite naughty at times. Us Littles are meant to be the naughty ones.'

For a moment, before she realizes what she's said, she looks the happiest I've ever seen her. Then, she covers her hand with her mouth and looks deeply upset.

'It's OK,' I say, reaching up towards her. 'You don't need to be ashamed. There's nothing wrong with it. It's natural. It's who you are.'

She smiles, grimly. 'I just, I'm not used to people knowing, that's all.'

'Don't worry,' I nod. 'I get it. I've met other Littles. Quite a few. Not everyone's totally open about who they are. But at least you know who you are. Lots of people don't.'

'Sometimes I wish I wasn't a Little.' She looks so sad. She's been through something awful, I can tell. That's something that we've got in common.

'I understand that. But you know what? I'm glad you are. Hey, I've got an idea. If you're a good girl today — no cussing, no breaking any rules — then later you can teach me how to bake. I'll even wear an apron.'

Harper claps her hands together excitedly. 'Ooooh please please please!'

'Good.'

She smiles. 'So, what are we getting for breakfast?'

'How bout we get.... outta here?'

CHAPTER TEN

She groans. 'OK, you're definitely a Daddy, cause that was the biggest dad joke I ever heard in my life.'

I crack my knuckles. 'Kid, you ain't seen nothing yet.'

*

I always love to ride my bike, but this ride is like no other. To have Harper on here, sharing one of the great passions of my life, is fucking great.

She clings on to me from behind, holding tight as I accelerate and break, turn and rev. Each time the engine steps up a gear, I hear this tiny little whoop of excitement from behind.

By the time we get to Pann's Restaurant, I kinda wish we had further to go — I don't want her to let go.

'Oooh, I've never been here, but I've always wanted to come.'

Pann's is a Los Angeles institution. Been around since the 1950s and it's a totally iconic place. The servers all wear old-timey 1950s-style outfits, and the whole place is decked out as though is hasn't changed in the seventy or so years since it opened.

We're ushered inside and we sit by the window, looking out at the busy street. There's old-time rock and roll playing on the jukebox and the atmosphere is buzzing. It's an old cliché that it can feel like everyone in LA is involved in the movie business, but in here, right now, I'd be willing to bet that most of the patrons actually are.

There are meetings going on left and right, with beautiful people discussing scripts and casting calls left right and center.

'My friend, Felicity, comes here all the time,' Harper says, her eyes wide as she takes in the menu.

'Oh yeah?'

'She works for a movie studio — Galactic. Just an assistant, but she's writing scripts.'

'I'd love to meet her.'

She looks surprised. 'You wanna meet my friends?'

'Sweetheart, maybe you don't get it yet,' I say, dropping my guard. 'I kinda like you, and I wanna know everything there is to know about you.'

Her cheeks pinken, and she hides behind the menu.

'You're making me blush,' she says, her voice muffled.

'Good,' I growl. 'Now let's eat. I'm buying. Choose anything you want. Except salad. I need you to eat a nice, big breakfast.'

'Anything *except* salad?'

'Oh yeah, no cake, either. We might be having that later.'

'Hmmm, all these choices.' She pushes a finger to her lips, considering carefully. 'I mean, obviously I'm gonna have waffles.'

'Obviously,' I say.

'But the question is, what type of chicken do I have with them? Leg, thigh, wing...?'

'Have the thigh. It's the best part. No question.' I speak with authority.

She looks excited to have me choose. 'OK, sounds good. What about you?'

'I'm having salad.'

She looks disgusted. 'No way!'

I grin, laugh. 'I'm kidding, sheesh. Nah, I'm having country fried steak with hash browns and grits. A man breakfast.'

'Caveman breakfast, more like,' she smiles.

'Hey, watch that attitude,' I say.

'Sorry Daddy,' she says. It's like she's reacting on instinct, like she's

CHAPTER TEN

not really in control of what she's saying. And that's the way I like it. I don't make a big deal about the fact that she called me Daddy — Hawk told me not to — but inside, my heart's going berserk.

'That's OK, sweetheart,' I reply. 'I'll let you off.'

We order the food from a friendly young woman with a bright red hat and a bright white smile, and as we wait for our breakfast to arrive, I figure it's a good time to probe a little more into Harper's history.

'So, I've never had a relationship with a Little before.' It takes courage to use the 'r' word. I don't even know if she feels attracted to me. Maybe this is just a sub/care-giver relationship. Platonic. Non-sexual. I hope not, but it's hard to feel as though she digs me. She's so perfect and I'm so... me.

'And I've never had a Daddy before.'

'So, it's kinda like the blind leading the blind. I've been reading up on it though, chatting to friends who know what they're doing.'

'Nice of you to study up.'

'I think we should go over some ground rules. And they need to come from you. The other day, you said you struggle with cussing. So I suggest we keep that rule. No cussing.'

'Sounds f.......ricking good,' she says, looking me in the eye as she avoids the swear word.

'Maybe rule two should be no pushing your luck.'

She laughs. 'If that was a rule, I'd pretty much be constantly punished for the rest of my life.'

It's so good to talk to her, so easy. I wonder if she feels the same. It seems like she's totally at ease, so hopefully she's enjoying opening up to me.

'OK, let's dodge that one. What do you want to work on?'

'Hmmm,' she says. 'Trouble is I'm so perfect already. I'm just kidding. You know what, actually, I want help with confidence. It's never been my strong suit. But recently, I've just been. I don't know. Mopey. And I criticize myself, like, all the time. In my head, constantly.'

'OK. Well, how's this. I want you to be nice to yourself. And I don't just mean no self-criticism. I mean I want you to try some affirmations.'

'Affirmations?'

'Every day, when you wake up, and before you go to sleep, you're gonna say one thing about yourself that you like, while you look in the mirror. Then, when you're done, I want you to tell me what you said.'

'What if I can't think of anything,' she says, looking down at her hands.

'I'll help you. Don't worry.'

'OK then. That sounds like a good rule.'

'There's one more thing,' I say. I'm not even sure about the next one, myself. But something's telling me that it's important.

'Go on.'

'I want to take things slow. You know. If anything romantic *does* happen between us. And I'm not saying it has to, or anything like that. I just... I don't wanna waste this opportunity by taking things too fast.'

She smiles. 'I like that.'

'Good.'

The server swoops in with plates full of food for us. It smells sensational.

'My mouth is literally watering,' says Harper. 'I feel like someone in a cartoon.'

'Tuck in!' I say, cutting into the chicken fried steak.

'Oh my god this tastes so insanely good!' she says.

'I guess that chicken plus waffles plus maple syrup is pretty dang delicious,' I say.

CHAPTER TEN

'Who'd have thought it! I wonder if I can work this into a cake recipe.'

'Chicken cake?' I say, uncertain.

'OK, maybe not chicken. But like, maple-bacon?'

We eat happily for a couple minutes. Then an idea hits me. It's big, and it's exciting, and I immediately want to share it with Harper. But I don't want to overburden her. I'll have to show her slowly.

'You really want to be a baker, don't you?'

'Mmhmm. Or a professional eater,' she grins.

'How about this for an idea: I'm gonna help you with a business plan.'

'A business plan?'

'Yeah. It'll be boring — lots of math and marketing stuff — but if we work together, maybe you won't need Frank and Superstar Frosting to realize your baking dreams.'

'You think I could do it?' Her eyes are so full of hope and gratitude.

'I know you can do it,' I reply.

'Dane, I really like that you believe in me. It makes me feel... like I'm worth something.'

I reach out and touch her hand. 'You're worth a lot, Harper. An absolute fuckton.'

'Hey! You're allowed to cuss?'

'You bet your sweet ass I'm allowed to cuss.'

'So unfair!'

'Life's unfair, sweetheart, life's unfair.' I lean back in my chair. 'There's one more thing I'd like to ask you, Harper. And you can say no if you want. This is all an experiment, and we're learning together after all.'

'What is it?'

'I'd like you to call me Daddy. Like, all the time.'

She lifts a chicken thigh to her lips, and bites heartily into it. Somehow, it's the sexiest thing I've just about ever seen. 'I think I can manage that, Daddy,' she says.

'You know what?' I say. 'I think you've been a really good girl today. You deserve a special treat.'

'I know *exactly* what I want, Daddy,' she replies, a devilish look in her eye.

CHAPTER ELEVEN

HARPER

'Come on!' I squeal. 'Come out, I wanna see how you look!'

It's late in the afternoon, and Dane and I are back at my place. He's in the bathroom, getting changed.

'I don't know if I can come out,' he says, his voice all growly and nervous at the same time. 'I don't know how I figured that this would ever be a good idea.'

'Come on Daddy, you're brave, I won't think anything bad of you.'

'Promise?'

'Of course,' I say, giggling under my breath. I look out across the kitchen counter. I've got everything ready for Dane. Flour, eggs, butter, sugar. Cake tins and mixing bowls.

'OK, I'm coming out. Ready or not, here I come.'

The bathroom door swings open and out steps Dane.

Holy shit.

He's wearing an apron. And nothing else on top.

My mouth drops open. I knew he was gonna be wearing the apron, but I hadn't expected him to be shirtless beneath.

'Daddy!' I gasp.

'How do I look? You think that the boys in the club would mind if I showed up to the next meeting like this?'

Well, I mean he looks ridiculously good. I never thought that a man wearing an apron would do this to me. I can see his arms and his chest, so thick and heavy with muscle. Tattoos are wrapped around his torso and are across his shoulders.

The apron, a bright white, contrasts deliciously with his tan skin. I look further down his body, find myself wishing that he wasn't wearing any pants either. The thought of seeing the weight of his cock, pushing up against the fabric is doing funny things to my insides.

'You know that you're meant to be wearing a t-shirt or something underneath that thing?'

He gives me an innocent look. 'Oops. I'm so new to the whole baking game, I didn't even realize. What a dumb mistake.'

I narrow my eyes, not entirely convinced that it's possible for a fully-grown man to go through life not knowing how people wear aprons.

'Yes,' I say, my eyes still narrow. 'What a *mistake*.'

'You don't think I'd do something like this on purpose, do you?' he asks, slyly. 'I'm trying to set you a good example, now that I'm acting as your Daddy.'

'A good example, huh?' I say, biting my lip.

'Would you like me to go put a top on?' he asks, gesturing back to the bathroom.

'No!' I say, a little bit too quickly. 'I mean, no thanks, Daddy. It's getting late and we need to get this cake baked before bedtime.'

He walks over to the counter. 'We haven't even spoken about bedtime yet, have we Baba?'

I can't help but grin when he calls me that. It's so nice to hear his stern voice being so kind and tender. 'So does that mean I can stay up as late as I like?'

'Naughty,' he says. 'You know, I still owe you a punishment for your cussing the other day.'

I feel my chest tighten. So he hasn't forgotten.

'What time should I go to bed?'

'I think no later than ten is a decent idea. And we'll have story time before then, if you like? How does that sound?'

CHAPTER ELEVEN

Story time sounds super, super great. But I'm not used to going to bed that early. I decide to try my luck. 'What about ten thirty?' I ask.

Dane puts his hands on his hips, and shakes his head. If you're in bed by ten, that means you can get up at six and still get a good eight hours sleep.'

'Do *you* get eight hours sleep a night?' I ask.

'That's irrelevant,' he says, shaking his head. 'I'm not the one looking to start a new business. You need to be fresh and ready for whatever the day may throw at you.'

'OK,' I say, grumpy. 'But the story better be really good.'

'Oh, it'll be good,' he smiles. 'Really, really good. Now, are you gonna teach me how to bake, or what?'

*

It's not a date, I keep telling myself. You're just a Little, and he's just being your Daddy, and you're just playing silly games in the kitchen together and it's *not a date*.

'Is it meant to be this goopy?' He holds up a wooden spoon that's totally covered in cake batter. It doesn't just look goopy. I can tell by the strange, uneven consistency that he didn't sieve his flour, but I decide to play a little trick on him.

'Oh yeah,' I say, smiling innocently. 'That's just perfect, Daddy. It's gonna turn out great.'

'Why is it that I'm having trouble believing you today, young lady?'

He returns his spoon to the batter and starts beating it.

'You know,' he continues, 'I can see why you enjoy this.'

'Baking, or going topless with just an apron.'

'Both,' he grins. When he smiles, his whole face changes. There's always a rugged, handsome quality to his harsh looks, but when he smiles it just makes me want to swoon. 'But mainly the baking.'

'I'm glad you're enjoying it.'

'It's actually a pretty good work out.'

I snort with laughter. 'Not for a big strong man like you, surely?'

He curls his lip, beats the batter again. 'Must be using muscles I don't use too often. Not every day that I whip batter for so long.'

'Can't wait to see how you handle the piping,' I say. My cake's already in the oven, and it's starting to smell heavenly in here. I used some orange rind and rose water in the batter. Hopefully the flavors will come across when the cake's ready to eat.

I watch him as he stirs his mix, marveling at the way his body moves, at the way his muscles drive his powerful arms. Damn, I kinda wish I was the batter, and he was whipping *me*...

'You mind if I ask you a question, Harper?'

'Nope,' I say. I peek through the oven door. Looks like the cake's rising nicely. 'Ask away.'

'What's your history, you know, with age play?'

My heart starts to pound. My defenses go up. 'Uh. I dunno.' My voice is quiet.

'Hard to talk about?'

I nod, keep my eyes down.

'I get it,' he says. He puts the bowl down on the table in front of him, claps his hands together, sending flour flying in every direction. 'Just want you to know, this is a safe space. And I'm not talking about your place. I mean, wherever we are — me and you — that's a safe space. No judgment. No prejudice. Whatever you want to share, I'll accept it, and I promise I won't think badly of you.'

'You promise?'

CHAPTER ELEVEN

My voice is uncertain.

'Come here,' he says, holding out his hand to me. I bashfully approach, holding out my own hand. When I'm close, he sticks out his pinkie. 'I pinkie promise.'

I grin, slip my pinkie finger into his, then we squeeze each other's fingers tight. I can feel a warmth between us, as he keeps hold of me, like he's letting me know that everything's gonna be alright.

'Well,' I say. 'I've kinda known since school. That something about me was different.'

'For a while, huh?'

'Mmhmm. I had this best friend, at school — Laura — she taught me about it. Showed me some websites and stuff.'

'She was a Little, too?'

The pain of thinking about Laura is almost too much to bear. 'I thought she was,' I say.

He looks at me, concerned, then he squeezes my hand in his again, letting his palm rest on top of my knuckles. 'What happened, Baba?'

With his whispered words, I'm back there. Back in school.

'I was sixteen,' I say, my voice, tiny, vulnerable. 'Me and Laura had been talking about Little stuff for months. We had sleepovers, and we'd wear onesies and play with stuffies and do coloring and stuff. It was the happiest time of my life.'

'Sounds wonderful,' Dane says, his voice full of genuine tenderness.

'It was. Even though Laura was my only friend, I was happy. I even hoped that one day, I'd be able to tell my parents about how different I was, and I could be open about my identity. Laura was never like that though. I always felt like she was ashamed. Her big sister, Yasmine, was one of the most popular girls in school. She was kind of a bully. Used to call me names. She didn't know that I was a Little, but she knew I was different. And that was enough.'

Dane nods. 'School was a long time ago for me. But I fucking hated it. Being different sucks.'

I wonder for a second how someone like Dane could have been anything other than the most popular kid in school, but I guess I don't know him that well. I wonder what made his time in school so hard.

'Anyway, keep going,' Dane says. 'I didn't mean to butt in.'

'Well, me and Laura had been talking for a while about... diaper stuff.'

'Diapers eh?' He lifts an eyebrow. 'Some of the girls at the club wear them. But they're not for everyone.'

'Yeah, well, I was never that into the idea, but for some reason, Laura really *wanted* me to try wearing them.'

Dane looks confused. 'But why did she care what you wore?'

I sigh.

'One day, at school, she told me to meet her in the bathroom. She was waiting for me with a diaper. She bought it on-line for me. I tried to tell her that I didn't really feel comfortable wearing it, but she wouldn't listen, kept telling me how cute I'd look and that she bought it specially for me.'

'Peer pressure.' He grunts.

'Extreme peer pressure. I'd never said no to anything that Laura had said to me before. How could I say no to this? She was my only friend.' I pause a moment. 'She was my safe space.'

He squeezes my hand again.

'So I put it on. She waited outside the cubicle, told me to come out so that she could see. I'll never forget how the diaper felt against my skin — so crinkly and plasticy. It was so crinkly that I didn't hear everyone come in.'

CHAPTER ELEVEN

'Oh no...' gasps Dane.

'When I opened the cubicle, Yasmine was there, with all her friends. I froze, my diapers clearly on display. And she took a picture. It was one of those old-fashioned polaroid cameras. Everyone was laughing. Even Laura. I jumped back inside the cubicle. Locked it tight. But it was too late.'

'You poor thing.'

I feel the tears coming now, hot and wet against my cheeks. 'While I was in there,' I sniff, 'crying my eyes out, I promised that I'd never tell anyone that I was a Little, ever again.'

'I'm sorry,' he says, quietly. 'No-one should have to go through something like that.'

I'm crying hard now, and I feel instantly self-conscious, but I can't stop.

'Being there wasn't the bad part,' I heave. 'The bad part was knowing that my parents would find out. And knowing that there wouldn't be another day at school when I wouldn't get teased. And why wouldn't they tease me? I'm a freak!'

'Hey,' says Dane, quietly but firmly, 'you're not a freak. And I don't want to hear you say that. Your feelings aren't bad, I totally understand why you feel the way you do. But when you act on them by criticizing yourself, you make things worse. I promise.'

I sniff, nod. I can feel my face, all hot and wet, and I dread to think what Dane must be thinking. 'Please don't look at me,' I say, wiping my nose with my arm.

'Why?'

'Because I'm disgusting.'

I feel his hand under my chin. He lifts my face up so that I'm looking straight at him.

'I don't want to hear you say that again,' he says. His voice is soft, there's no meanness. 'Because you're the most wonderful, gorgeous creature I've ever seen.'

My heart starts to beat faster, my skin feels clammy.

'And you're no freak, Harper. You're a human being, like anyone else. If you're a freak, then I'm king of the freaks.'

Did he call me gorgeous?

'Now,' he says, 'I want you to do something for me.'

'What?' I whisper.

'I want you to kiss me.'

'Even though…?' I point at myself.

He smiles. 'You think that a big, tough guy like me is gonna let some snot and tears put me off? Baby, you've got a lot to learn about me.'

And just before his lips meet mine, my tears fade away, and I feel myself smile.

It's soft, first. Slow and gentle. Like he's feeling me out. He pulls me in close, and tenderly kisses my lips once, twice, three times. Then, it's like he's tasted something he likes, and all of a sudden, he's starving for me. He draws me in with a grunt, twists me round and pushes himself expertly against me. I feel his strength, his dominance, his power come through with every move, and as his tongue explores my mouth, I'm lost to him. I belong to him.

When he pulls away, I'm dazed, still lost, still remembering the kiss.

'Peanut butter cups,' I say.

'Excuse me?' his faces twists into an insane smile.

'I don't even know.' I say. 'Wow. That was something.'

'It really was.'

'It was like we just-'

'Fit together.'

CHAPTER ELEVEN

'Did you just finish my-'

'Sausages?' he asks, a playful grin on his face.

I return the grin. Then, I realize something. I feel amazing. And not just because of the kiss. I feel like a huge weight's been lifted from my shoulders. I feel like I'm finally free.

'OK,' he says. 'Now, I'd love to do that again. A lot. But, I think I can smell something burning.'

My eyes snap wide open. 'Eeeeeek!'

CHAPTER TWELVE

DANE

Man, it feels good to wake up in a damn bed. I'm lying, fully clothed — well, except for the apron I wore yesterday — next to Harper. She's still asleep, and she looks wonderful, like some sort of sleep Goddess. Her chest rises and falls with each breath, her eyelids occasionally flickering.

We only kissed once last night, but it felt like with that tiny release of tension, everything got better. The rest of the evening was spent laughing and joking, mostly finishing each other's sausages, and eating way too much fucking cake.

I mean, look, I like cake as much as the next man, and Harper's was insanely delicious, but mine was not so good. Dry, but at the same time, weirdly undercooked, I still ate some, mainly to get a laugh out of Harper. To be honest, I'd eat just about fucking anything if it got a laugh out of that girl.

Man, what are the guys in the club gonna say when I tell them what's going on? That I've fallen for a fucking Little. I know what Hawk will say. He's been telling me I'm a natural Daddy Dom for years. Don't know why I've resisted for so long.

Actually, fuck that, I know exactly why. I *hate* being told what to do.

I stroke a stray hair away from Harper's cheek. Poor girl deserves a lie-in, the amount of shit she's been through recently. Actually, by the sound of her story yesterday, she's been going through shit her whole life.

Now I've had my fair share of problems, but public humiliation isn't something I've ever experienced. At least not on that scale.

Last night, before we went to sleep, Harper came up to me and said, 'Daddy, I think I'm ready for my affirmation.'

I felt so damn proud. She told me that she wanted me to watch her the first time.

So I stood behind her as she looked into the bathroom mirror.

'I'm not a freak.' She said, then she turned around and hugged me tight as she could.

'Hey, do one more for me,' I said, before whispering in her ear.

She turned bright red then looked into the mirror.

'And my Daddy says I'm a very good kisser!' Then she shrieked with laughter and ran into bed.

I smile with pride. The urge to lean over and kiss Harper on the forehead is so strong. Should probably hold back though. She was so emotionally vulnerable last night, I kinda felt bad kissing her. I don't want her to feel pressured into anything at all.

Seeing her like that though, so open, and so deserving of affection, I couldn't stop myself. I hope she doesn't wake up this morning and regret that we kissed.

Nothing happened in the night, of course. I just wanted to keep her company in bed.

Bud's gonna give me hell for this. 'You mean you were in her fucking bed and nothing happened? Where's the boy I raised?'

Like I say, he's got kinda old-fashioned opinions when it comes to women.

'I can see you smiling.' Harper's voice sounds truly naughty this morning.

'I didn't know you were awake.' I say, as she opens her eyes.

'I've been watching you, Daddy. Planning. Waiting patiently. Biding my time.'

CHAPTER TWELVE

She's in a frisky mood this morning.

'Have you indeed?'

'Uh-huh. And now is my time to strike!' She jumps up, clutching a pillow, and brings it down over my head.

'No!' I cry, 'My one weakness! Pillows!'

She gurgles a laugh out and then wraps her arms around my neck. 'Daddy,' she says, 'can I ask you something.'

'Of course.'

'You know we only kissed like, once last night.'

Damn. I hope she hasn't been worried all night about this. 'Yep,' I say.

'Is it because you never ever ever want to kiss my gross lips ever again?' She's smiling, playing with me. I love her like this. So free and happy.

'That's it,' I say. 'You got me. My evil plan to never kiss you again. You worked it out.'

'Mwahahaha. And now, it's time to strike.'

I'm expecting the kiss, but I'm not expecting a kiss like this. It starts out as a joke, as a messy fumble of lips, but within seconds, I feel Harper's hands, hungry for me, wrapped around my body. She digs her fingers into the muscle of my back, and it's driving me wild.

I growl, hug her in tight, then as I pushed my tongue to hers, our bodies meet — her softness against my hard. She moans as I bite her lip, she sighs as I slip my hand down her panties, feeling the softness of her ass.

'Oh fuck,' she says, whimpering as I kiss her throat.

'No fucking cussing,' I say.

'Oh no!' she gasps, as I pull her in close.

'That won't save you,' I say. 'You've broken my rules one too many times, Babygirl, and now you're gonna feel my palm across your backside.'

She shivers with lust.

'First though, give me a safe-word. You're in control.'

'Danger,' she says, biting her lip.

'I like it,' I say. 'Now tell me, in the bedroom, how much control do you want to give away?'

'All of it,' she says, giving me the dirtiest look I've ever seen.

'You OK with bondage? Bum stuff?' I run through the checklist Hawk told me the other day.

She nods, hungrily. 'Just tell me what you're doing, before you do it. Oh, no choking — that's scary.'

'Sure thing, baby. No choking at all, I promise. Remember, you're in control. If you think of anything else, you use that safe word and let me know. I won't think badly of you for it. Now, it's time to tan your hide.'

She shrieks, 'I'm sorry, Daddy, please don't spank me.

No safe word. That means I'm in control. So, I pull those panties down, and grit my teeth. Then, before I can do anything else, there's a knock at the door. It's loud, and instantly seems rude.

'Ignore it,' she whispers.

But the knocks continue. 'Harper, I know you're in there.' Fuck. It's Frank. 'If you want to keep your job, you'll come out here right now!'

'Oh no!' Harper hisses.

'Don't worry, Baby. See what he wants. I'll hide in the bathroom, but I'll be listening. Anything funny goes down, I'll be out in a second.'

She looks at me, a little scared for a moment, then she nods. 'OK. You better hide.' She gives me a quick kiss on the lips — it's good, but I want so much more. Then, she looks at the door. 'Coming!' She cries

CHAPTER TWELVE

out. 'I overslept.'

'Course you did,' comes the muffled reply.

I rush into the bathroom and pull the door so that it's almost closed. I should be able to hear through this just fine, and if I need to rush out, that won't be a problem.

In fact, if I hold my eye up to the crack, I can just about see the front door. I watch as Harper pulls on a pair of joggers. Of course I'm staring at her ass — where else would I be looking? I'm still full of lust at the moment, and just knowing that I had my hands all over her just a moment ago is driving me wild.

Harper opens the door and I see Frank for the first time. Guy does not look good. Short, hairy, and angry-looking. People who've been angry their whole life have this particular look, like their eyes are stuck in a permanent scowl. That's Frank's face.

'Thanks for keeping me waiting,' he says.

I'm instantly furious. The way he's talking to Harper is disgusting.

'Sorry,' she says.

'What kept you?'

'Like I said, I overslept.'

This piece of dirt doesn't deserve her politeness. It takes all my effort not to burst out and wring his scrawny neck.

'Whatever. I've got another job for you. He steps to the side. There's a stack of cake boxes behind him. 'I want these delivered to the same location you went to the other day.'

'Today?' I can hear the disappointment in her voice.

'Of course today. You think cakes are gonna keep overnight? They need to be fresh, dumb-ass, or our clients will be furious. I know you don't care about our clients, but I fucking do.'

This guy is obviously an asshole, but he doesn't necessarily strike me as a criminal. I wonder how a fucking baker got involved with drug smuggling in Los Angeles. Hopefully soon, I'll be able to find.

'So, it's the same client as the other day? They want more of these cakes?'

He gives her a searing look, and I know why. She's not dumb. She's trying to get more information for her. It's a smart thing to do, but also risky as fuck, and as proud as I am, I kinda wish she'd kept her mouth shut.

'Don't worry about it,' he says. 'Your job isn't to think. And your job isn't to ask questions. The only reason you're still getting paid is because you haven't fucked up a delivery. Yet. Now get dressed, and get these cakes to San Pedro.'

Without saying goodbye, without helping to carry the cake boxes across the threshold, he just leaves.

What a piece of work.

Harper's just standing by the door. She obviously doesn't know what to do. She glances back at the bathroom, then looks out the door, making sure that Frank's gone. Then she grabs the boxes and starts to move them into her apartment.

'Hey, let me help you,' I say, emerging from my bathroom prison. 'That guy is a fucking jerk.'

'He never used to be like this,' she says, carrying two cake boxes onto the kitchen table.

'I wonder what happened to him,' I say. 'He's obviously in debt to someone or something. You can tell by how badly he's treating you, that someone else is treating him really shitty.'

She pauses. 'You think so?'

'Course,' I say, taking one of the boxes. 'Shittiness is a cycle. You learn it from other people. Sometimes, your parents are shitty to you,

CHAPTER TWELVE

and so you learn to be shitty to others. Sometimes it's a romantic partner, or a friend, or a business associate.'

'But people have been sh... nasty to me,' she says, correcting herself. 'Does that mean I'm gonna be shitty to other people?'

I shake my head. 'No. It's not guaranteed. But it takes a pretty damn special person to break the cycle. I guess that must mean that you're pretty damn special.'

Her cheeks flush pink again. I'll never get tired of seeing it.

'So, what are we gonna to do with these cakes? Call the police?'

I snort. 'You've gotta be kidding me. You think the cops would help?'

'So, what? I'm just gonna have to deliver them? I'm trapped in this job?'

I shake my head. 'Absolutely not. I've got a plan.'

'A plan?' she asks, looking uncertain.

'Yep. This idiot's just delivered us the key to this whole thing.'

'So what are we gonna do?'

'Well first,' I say, opening a cake box up, 'we're gonna do some more baking. After that, I've got a phone call to make.'

'More baking? I don't understand.'

The cake inside the box is small, and covered in thick buttercream. I test the weight. Yep, it's suspiciously heavy.

'Harper,' I say, 'you think you can bake a cake exactly like this one? Iced like this too?'

She snorts. 'Easy peasy.'

'How long you think it'll take?'

'Not too long. Hour and a half?'

I take out my phone. 'Great. That should give Rip plenty of time to get over here.'

LUCKY MOON

'Rip's coming? The doctor.'
'Oh,' I say, 'he's more than just a doctor.'

CHAPTER THIRTEEN

HARPER

'Shouldn't we be using a knife for this?'

Dane holds the spoon up to the light. 'You only cut cake with a knife when you don't care about harming what's inside.'

'I thought Harper was the cake expert.' That's Rip. He's standing nearby, with his arms crossed across his chest, a sardonic grin on his face.

'She is,' snorts Dane. 'But I'm the expert in cutting shit up with knives.'

I can't help but laugh.

'So what's gonna be inside?' I ask. I don't know why, but I'm seriously damn anxious about this. I'm half expecting a jack-in-the-box to pop out, or some insanely scary killer clown to surprise me.

'Well,' he says, pushing the edge of the spoon down into the buttercream frosting. 'I think there's gonna be some cake in here. But I also think that there's gonna be quite a lot of drugs.'

He pushes the spoon further in, until, after a couple of seconds, it stops.

'You hit something?' I ask, my voice practically a whisper.

He nods. Then, with a flourish, he pulls the sponge and buttercream to the side, revealing a smooth, white rectangle.

'I suspected this is what we were dealing with,' Dane says. 'But there's something especially diabolical about seeing it in the flesh.'

'In the sponge,' grunts Ripper.

'That's it. Imagine baking a brick of cocaine into a fucking cake.'

'It's smart, actually,' says Rip. 'Sniffer dogs would probably just smell the cake. Be at least confused for a while. Give the smuggler a chance to get through customs or whatever.'

'You think?' Dane asks, looking skeptical.

'I dunno,' Ripper replies with a smile. 'I'm a doctor, not a veterinarian.'

Even though Dane and Ripper seem confident and are joking together, I'm still feeling super nervous. It's not just because I've been worried about what's gonna be inside the cake. No. I'm worried about what I'm gonna have to do later on. The delivery.

'S-so, how much is that worth?' I ask, eying up the brick of cocaine that Dane's casually handling. I think it's the first time I've ever actually seen any type of drug in real life, even though

'This?' he asks. 'If this is pure, the way I expect it to be, then it could be worth about...' he purses his lips, 'ten grand? Maybe. Maybe more?'

My eyes nearly pop out of my head. Ten thousand dollars. 'That's insane,' I gasp.

Dane grins. 'I know seems nuts doesn't it. This simple white powder's worth so much. I wonder how much a pound of flour is worth.'

'Forty-three cents,' I say, almost as quick and precise as a robot.

'You little flour nerd,' Dane says, with no malice in his voice. 'So do you think if we replaced the cocaine inside these cakes with flour, our friends would be upset?'

My eyes widen. 'Won't they know?' I ask.

'How?' he replies. 'They aren't gonna open up the cakes when you deliver them. And if they did, they'd just see a hard brick of white powder.'

'What you gonna do with the blow?' Ripper asks.

'Keep it safe,' Dane replies. 'Then when this is all over, I'll make an

CHAPTER THIRTEEN

anonymous call to the LAPD.'

'Not before?' Ripper says. 'Why not hand it over now.'

'Cause there's a chance they'll track me down. And if they do that, I won't be able to bring the Blood Fuckers down.'

'That's your plan? Bring down the whole organization? Dane, you need to be careful.' There's caution in Rip's voice.

'Don't worry, I know how to look after myself.'

'Daddy,' I say, my voice suddenly quiet. 'This is gonna sound like a disrespectful question.'

'It's OK,' Dane says. 'You can ask me whatever you need to.'

'Why do you care about this stuff?'

For a moment, he narrows his eyes.

'What I mean is,' I say, 'why don't you just leave it to the police to sort this stuff out? You don't take drugs. You're not a dealer, so it doesn't affect you that this stuff's on the streets. Couldn't I just quit the job and get on with my life?'

He nods. 'You could. It's just that I've got a kind of history with drugs. And just because they're not affecting me, doesn't mean that other innocent people aren't gonna get hurts. Addicts aren't the only victims of the drug trade.'

'Have you told her?' Rip asks. I wonder what he's talking about.

Dane shakes his head — such a quick movement I almost miss it.

'Tell me what?' I ask.

'Well. Drugs are how I ended up in Daddies MC.'

I'm shocked. 'You used to take drugs?'

He shakes his head. 'Nope. Not me. My folks. Like I say, the addicts aren't the only victims of the drug trade. Happened a long time ago now. When I was just a kid. Back in the eighties. My parents chose heroin over me. Abandoned me.'

My heart pounds. How could someone abandon a baby? I feel so many things — anger, sadness, terrible, icy horror. 'I'm so sorry,' I say.

'It's OK,' he says. 'I don't blame them. Woulda been worse if they'd kept me. I'd have ended up dead, most likely. Or worse. An addict myself. Instead, I ended up in the foster system. Spent years hoping to be adopted. But I was a troublemaker. Families didn't want me. I don't blame them for that either.'

He's speaking dispassionately, as though he's talking about something that happened to someone else. I know that the pain is still with him.

Now I get it. Why he was talking about being different at school. He must have changed schools quicker than I change panties. And new kids get it harder than anyone.

'Finally, I pushed things too far. Got in serious trouble. Started running drugs myself. Thought that my life had been ruined by fucking narcotics, so why shouldn't I make some money out of the damn things. All I got was a stretch of jail time.'

'You poor thing,' I say putting a hand on his arm.

'When I got out, I didn't know what to do. Didn't have anywhere to turn. I was an angry young man with no future. Then I met Bud. The rest is history.'

'Who's Bud?' I ask.

'President of Daddies MC. Old-fashioned guy, but he's got a good heart. He helped me. Turned me into the man I am today. Taught me responsibility and love. I owe him everything.'

'Wow,' I say, 'he must be an amazing guy.'

I finally understand Dane's crusade against drugs. And there's no way I'm gonna let him down.

'Can't we just arrest Darlin' and all the other gangsters at the

CHAPTER THIRTEEN

warehouse. You know, not arrest maybe, but like, beat them up?'

Dane smiles. 'I like it when you try to be tough, Harper. You stick your tongue out in the cutest way imaginable.'

Damn him for making me blush all the time.

'In answer to your question, we're not after Darlin'. She's a small fry. We want a guy who calls himself Satan — the head of the blood fuckers.'

'Satan?' I gulp. 'He sounds... nice.'

'He's not. But no-one knows who he is, and no-one knows where he's based.'

'So if we give them the flour,' I say, 'that'll just make them mad, right. How are we gonna find them?'

'*We* aren't gonna do anything,' Dane says. 'You're gonna be safely away from the situation. I'm gonna be the one handling this thing.'

'I didn't mean that-'

'I know Baba, I just want you to know that you're safe. I'm gonna look after you, no matter what.'

My heart fills with warm, snuggly feelings. 'Thank you, Daddy,' I say.

Ripper gives Dane and me a look. 'You two are good together,' he says. 'I'm happy for you.' His smile is genuine and sweet. I really like Rip.

'You soppy old ass,' Dane says, shaking his head.

'Hey, don't insult my ass,' Rip says. 'I do a lot of work in the gym, I'll have you know. My butt's hard as a rock.'

I can't help but snort with laughter.

'Much as I love to discuss your exceptional physique, Rip, let's get back to the matter in hand. Did you bring the bug?'

'Sure I did.'

Rip passes something small to Dane, who shows it to me. 'This is how we're gonna track down the fuckers. It's a tracker.'

He passes it to me. It just looks like a tiny microchip, about the size of half a fingernail.

'This'll tell you where the cakes are going?'

Dane nods. 'To a range of accuracy of around half a foot.'

'So we put it inside the cake?'

'That's the plan.'

'How did you get this, Rip?' I ask. I'm fascinated by these men. Before I met them, I had a really specific view of bikers. I never would have imagined this strange, secret world of vigilante crime-busting, and spy-level gadgetry.

'Oh, I've got connections. Was a military medic for many years before my retirement. Special forces. Still know a couple guys in the service.'

'Special forces! Were you like a Navy SEAL?'

'If I told you that I'd have to kill you,' he says. 'Although I guess that goes against the Hippocratic oath. Even so, I better not tell you, just in case.'

Dane glances at the clock on my wall. 'Guys, I hate to break up the party, but we've got three cakes to ice in the next forty minutes. Then, our own special forces agent is going on her very first mission.'

I gulp.

Rip sees that I'm nervous. 'Don't worry sweetheart, we're gonna be watching. You'll be fine.'

'You're gonna come along too? Thanks Rip.'

'I wouldn't miss it for the world,' he says.

*

CHAPTER THIRTEEN

Even though Rip and Dane are following behind me on their motorbikes, I can't help but feel terrified as I approach the warehouse in San Pedro.

If I'd have known the other day that I was delivering drugs to a criminal, there's no way I would have completed the delivery. Now though, the only way I can stop myself from turning around is by imagining that I really am some secret, special forces super-soldier.

'Special Agent Harper,' I say to myself as I keep pedaling. 'Your mission, should you choose to accept it, is to infiltrate the compound of the evil Blood Fuckers.' Hehe, I can cuss as much as I want now that Dane can't hear me.

For just a second, I'm distracted, thinking of how good my Daddy's hands had felt on my butt as he kissed me in bed. It's such a powerful, visceral memory, that I feel my pussy start to tingle against my seat.

'Now's not the time for naughty thoughts, Special Agent Harper,' I say. 'No matter how strong and handsome and stud-like your Daddy may or may not be.'

I'm trying to keep myself cheerful, because I know that if I don't, I'm in danger of having a full-blown panic attack.

'Think about what Dane's been through. All you need to do is drop off the package, and get the heck out of there.'

Finally, I reach the warehouse. The plan is simple. Dane and Rip are gonna be watching nearby. If there's any trouble, or even a hint of trouble, all I need to do is scratch my ear with my right thumb, and they'll come running in to save me.

Otherwise, I'm on my own.

I chain up my bike and take my helmet off, looking behind me briefly. Obviously, Rip and Dane aren't visible, but I can't help myself.

LUCKY MOON

I unload the cakes. We only just managed to get all three baked and iced, and the drugs replaced with flour in time. It's late in the day. As I approach the front door, I have terrible thoughts flashing through my mind. Like they might just grab me. Or they might somehow know what we're planning and they might just shoot me.

Or they might open up a cake right in front of me.

But I know these things aren't going to happen. So I press the buzzer. And I wait.

CHAPTER FOURTEEN

DANE

'And then, and then, I just looked her straight in the eye, and, like, ice-cold, I said, 'Here's your cake. Hope you like frosting!' and she didn't even bat an eyelid. She was just like, whatever.'

'Baba, I'm so fucking proud of you, feels like the part of my brain responsible for pride is gonna damn burst.'

It's true. I'm really damn proud of Harper. But way more than pride, I'm feeling relief right now. The drop-off couldn't have gone better. Darlin' opened the door and grabbed the cakes without even really bothering to say anything to Harper.

When she realized she was in the clear — that we'd got away with it — Harper turned toward our general direction and gave this insane, goofy grin. Then she skipped all the way to her damn bike.

'I did a good job?' She squeezes my hand so hard that it feels like she's gonna cut off my circulation.

'You did,' I say. 'You know, for someone your size, you are just freakishly strong.'

We're walking down a dark alley on the way to The Milk Shed. I feel as though Harper's earned — at the very least — a drink tonight. I'm excited to show her this place, this part of my life. And I hope that she enjoys the 'special' Little services that we offer.

'It's my baker's arms.' She says. 'Got really strong wrist from all the —' she makes a motion that could be very easily misinterpreted.

'From all the jerkin' off?' I ask with a grin.

She punches my shoulder. 'No!' she gasps. 'All the kneading. Daddy, you're so naughty. Is s-e-x the only thing you ever think about?'

The way she spelled out the naughty word is fuckin' adorable. 'It's what I'm thinking about right now,' I growl.

She giggles. 'Is that so?'

'You're lucky that I can control myself. Dark, dirty alleys happen to be a big turn-on for me. If I weren't a responsible Daddy, you'd be in all sorts of trouble right now.'

'Ohhh, I bet this alley is real *dank* too,' she whispers, pushing her body into mine.

'It's real fucking dank, baby,' I say pulling her tight into me. 'Only problem is, because of your bravery and good behavior, I'm contractually bound to get you a drink this evening.'

'All these long words're making my head spin, Daddy.'

'I'll show you something that'll really make your head spin.'

I kiss her firmly, my lips pushing hers apart. She whimpers as I find her tongue, moans as our mouths talk without words. I grab her ass, pull her tight and then, just for a second, I push my fingers between her legs, touch her pussy through her clothes, and she writhes with pleasure, pushing herself hard into my fingers. I can feel the heat of her, so close. But for now, totally off limits.

I pull back.

'Come on, sweetheart, there's some folks I want you to meet.'

'Are we nearly there?'

'Honey, we're right on the fucking doorstep.'

She looks confused, and then she sees the door behind us. There, in tiny letters above the entrance, is the sign.

'You'd never know it was here,' she says.

'We don't exactly rely on passing trade,' I say, pushing open the door. 'We like to keep this a safe place for Daddies and Littles to come and express themselves. A lot of the people you'll see here are members

CHAPTER FOURTEEN

of Daddies MC, but plenty aren't.'

'I can't believe there's so much age play culture in LA that I don't know about,' she says, her eyes wide.

'Don't surprise me,' I reply, 'seeing as you haven't really been looking for it. Glad you're feeling less ashamed of yourself now.'

'I never thought I'd get to where I am.'

We walk into the reception area. Not many bars have one, but at The Milk Shed, you kind of have to know someone here to get in. Colette is standing behind the reception desk, her bright green hair shining in the dull light. In front of her sits Paulie, the club stuffie. He's a little yellow pug, tattered and threadbare after years of petting and cuddles from over-aggressive Littles.

'Hey Dane!' she says, her soft French accent instantly recognizable.

'Good to see you Colette,' I say. 'Busy night?'

'Not so much,' she says, looking down at the guest list. 'Just regulars. Nothing too heavy. And who's this cute little snack on your arm?'

Harper chuckles. 'I'm Harper,' she says, 'pleased to meet you!'

'Pleased to meet you Harper, I'm Colette. Is it your first time here?' Colette's talking so sweetly to Harper. She's always great with the new girls.

'Uh-huh.'

'You want me to go over the golden rule, sugar, or has your Daddy already explained it all to you?'

Harper looks up at me, with a mild look of worry.

'Is there a rule, Daddy?'

'It's no big deal, sweetheart. It's simple.' I gesture up to the wall behind Colette. Written on the wall, in child-like, bright, gold lettering are two words: No Judgement.

LUCKY MOON

'I think I'm gonna like this place,' Harper says, smiling.

'I hope so,' I say, 'because this place is basically me.'

'Then I know I'm gonna like it,' she adds, squeezing my hand again.

Colette steps out from behind the bar and walks up to the double doors. 'Harper,' she says, 'welcome to The Milk Shed.'

Then, she leans in, and pushes the swing-doors open. Harper's eyes widen, and are filled with reflections of the neon lights of the bar.

'Oh my god!' she gasps. 'This place is amazing!'

'You know what, I know that as the owner I'm biased, but I tend to agree with you.'

The idea for the decor here was to try to appeal to both hardcore bikers, and Littles. I know, sounds tricky, but in truth, it actually worked out pretty great.

There's the rare Harley behind the counter, but we've also got a display case for rare collectibles that the Littles would like. Stuffies, Pokémon cards, first editions of some popular children's books. We've got my privately sourced whiskey collection at the grown-up bar which Roxy manages, but we've also got an insane selection of juices and sodas from across the world — including some extremely unusual Japanese drinks which I feel as though Harper's gonna love.

Sure, we've got the heavy metal juke-box, but there's a Little party room where the girls and boys can go to bop along to sugary pop music for as long as they want.

Hawk is sitting with Rip — who left us a little early — at the bar. With them is Babs, Ripper's Little. Her long hair is dyed bright white, and it's braided into two thick plaits. She's wearing an old-fashioned pinafore dress. She's really into old Victorian fashion — wears all kinds of funky stuff. Not the kind of thing I'd ever think would look good, but somehow, it always looks natural on her. When she spies us from

CHAPTER FOURTEEN

across the room, she waves excitedly, and they all stand up.

Feels weirdly formal as we approach.

'I'm nervous Daddy,' Harper says.

'Don't be. I feel like you're gonna get on with these guys just great.'

'You must be Harper!' Babs says, clearly excited. 'I'm Babs, Ripper's girlfriend. I've heard so much about you!' She jumps forward, gives Harper a huge cuddle.

'That's such a nice cuddle,' says Harper, melting into Babs' warm embrace.

'I'm a professional cuddler!' Babs replies.

'Really?' says Harper.

'Oh you're too cute!' giggles Babs.

'She's a sports massage therapist,' Rip chips in. 'So it's not so much of a stretch to say she's a professional cuddler.'

'You're both very medical,' says Harper, still grinning. Don't think I've ever seen anyone grin as much in my life.

'I guess that's true,' says Rip, as he and Babs look at each other.

'This is Hawk,' I say, patting my friend on the shoulder.

'Good to meet you, sugar,' Hawk says, flashing her a grin. I'm way past being jealous of Hawk's looks, but I still wish I could smile like him.

'You too,' Harper replies.

'Hawk here is responsible for fixing up your bike.'

'It was nothing,' Hawk says, anticipating thanks.

'Maybe for you! My bike's never been better. I guess I owe all of you something.' She looks around the group. 'My guardian angels.'

'Fuck Dane,' says Hawk. 'You said she was cute, but you didn't tell me she was *this* fucking cute.'

'Hey,' Harper says, 'I owe all you guys. Can I buy you a round of drinks?'

'Harper,' I say, 'that's a lovely thought, but, why don't you let me buy a round of drinks. You can owe me for it. Pay me when you start your new business.'

'I just want to repay you all somehow,' she says, her face falling.

'You will,' I reply. 'Like I say, this is a loan. You'll owe me for it. So you're buying these drinks. Just right now, I happen to know that you need to focus on paying your rent. And as your care-giver right now, I can't allow you to spend money you can't afford.'

She nods. 'You're right.'

'Dane's a good guy,' Babs says.

'And by the looks of it, a natural Daddy,' says Hawk, seemingly impressed.

I hope I haven't undermined Harper, and made her feel small. I know how good it feels to buy drinks for people, and I hate the thought that she might be upset that I've taken her agency away from her.

I order drinks for everyone, then, as Roxy starts to put them together and everyone starts to chat, I lean in close to Harper and speak quietly, so that only she can hear me. 'Just remember, if there's *anything* I do or say that you don't like, say danger. It's not just a sexy times thing.'

She nods. 'I get it Daddy. Thank you for looking after me.' Then, she kisses me on the cheek, and I feel happy.

The chat flows freely, so do the drinks. Babs and Harper are on soft drinks, Rip and Hawk have a couple beers. I stick to water tonight — I need to get Harper safely home later. Not taking any chances. It feels like the most natural thing in the world.

'So what's your Little like?' says Babs, sucking through her straw.

'Um,' says Harper. 'I dunno. She's just... me I guess. She's a little bit

CHAPTER FOURTEEN

petulant. But mostly just wants to snuggle and be looked after.'

'Ugh, Babs' Little is a total brat!' Ripper says. 'Getting her to do as I say is a lifelong battle.'

'One that you love to fight, Daddy,' Babs says, turning on the charm, and batting her eyelashes at Ripper.

'She's right,' he says, holding his hands up. 'I *do* love it.'

'She walks all over you,' Hawk says. 'When was the last time you gave out a punishment.'

'Well,' says Ripper, 'there was that time you ate all the butterscotch and got spanked. When was that?'

Babs looks innocently. 'Oh was that a punishment?'

Hawk lets out a huge guffaw. 'You are so busted Rip. Handing out funishments instead of punishments.'

Ripper chuckles and nods. 'Maybe I am too soft on you. What's your take on discipline, Dane?'

I shake my head. 'We're just trying to work that out, aren't we sweetness.'

Harper nods. 'I think you've been really fair with me so far. Exactly what I need.' She squeezes my thigh under the table.

'Ahah, it's the gang!' I look up, and see Bud there. He's looking down at us. 'Who's this little lady.'

'This is Harper, Bud. The Little Girl I was telling you about.'

'You didn't tell me she was a fucking model!' Bud says. Sounds a little like he's slurring his words. Is he drunk? That is not his style. Or at least it never used to be. 'Nice to meet you darlin'. He leans in and hugs Harper.

'Nice to meet you, too, Bud,' she says. She gives me this weird look.

'So how's the crusade against drugs going, guys?' he says. 'You managed to stop the flow coming into our turf?'

'Not yet,' I say. 'But we've made major progress. Today was a big day.'

'Oh yeah?' he says, looking around as if to see if anyone's listening?

'We seized about forty grand's worth of blow.'

The look of shock on his face is a sight to behold. 'Forty grand's worth of blow? Are you fucking kidding me?' Then, a second later, he adds, 'That's amazing.'

'Yeah,' I say.

'And,' says Harper, 'we put—'

'Put their smuggling operation behind schedule,' I say, cutting in. Something's not right with Bud. I'm getting this feeling, and it's making me sick. All of a sudden, I'm starting to feel as though I might need to gather some more allies to me.

Fuck. That means contacting Rock. I've been putting it off for months. Maybe it's time.

'Anyway, Bud,' says Ripper, 'you wanna quick drink with us?'

'Nah,' says Bud. 'Got stuff to do. Can't have the president of the damn club drinking all night long.'

Just all day long? I don't ask.

As Bud leaves, Harper whispers to me. 'He's not really what I thought he'd be like.'

'Hmmm, me neither,' I reply. 'Harper,' I say, 'I'm tired, and I need to think. You wanna come back to mine tonight? We can leave the bike here.'

She looks at me with those gorgeous blue eyes. 'Have you got cocoa?' she replies.

'If that's what it'll take, I'll bring some back with us. Not gonna have you wanting for anything.'

She grins. 'Then I guess you can take me back to yours.'

CHAPTER FOURTEEN

I glance at Babs. 'She's rubbing off on you, isn't she?'
Harper looks scandalized. 'Daddy, how could you!?'
'Come on, you little brat-in-the-making, let's get you home.'

CHAPTER FIFTEEN

HARPER

OK, I can't remember the last time I was this excited. It's like the blood in my body's become carbonated, like I'm fizzing with an energy that I can't contain.

Complete a mission like a secret agent? Check.

Keep my cool under extreme pressure? Check.

Get invited into the most insanely cool secret bar in LA? Check.

And now, I'm riding back to the apartment of a gorgeous, tender Daddy who's gonna make me a cup of hot cocoa and help me get to sleep.

I can barely believe how much my life has changed in such a short amount of time. Ever since I rode into Dane's bike and landed on my butt, it's like I've been strapped to a roller coaster that I can't get off.

But to be honest, I don't want to get off it. I want to ride this all the way to the end.

Dane shifts up a gear and Angeline shoots forward with a throaty growl. I've got a motorbike helmet on, but that doesn't stop me feeling the wind in my hair. LA by night is an incredible experience. We're cruising down Sunset Boulevard, dodging between limos and cars, rolling past nightclubs and 24hr takeaways, past souvenir shops and bright-lit billboards. The horizon seems so wide and far away. Palm trees sway in the breeze, and I feel so free that if I stretch out my arms, I could take off and fly up high, straight up to the silvery moon.

We pull up to a set of lights, wait as a mass of pedestrians mill across the wide street.

'You OK back there?' Dane grunts, his voice only just audible over the roar of the engine.

'I'm perfect!' I cry back, giving his broad back another squeeze.

'Damn right you are,' he replies.

*

We stay out on the road a little longer. Dane shows me a couple of his favorite places — a rib place Downtown, and a coffee spot that he promises to take me to in a couple days.

'No science-lab barista shit in Marcy's,' he says as we roll past. 'Just fucking good filter, guaranteed.'

There's something about being on a motorbike that makes me feel insanely free. Feels like the world's our oyster. We can go wherever we want, as agile and light-footed as a cat.

Finally though, we pull up outside Dane's place. It's not much from the outside, but I can't wait to get in.

'Sorry I got you back so late, honey,' Dane says as he slips off the broad seat of the bike. 'Guess I got carried away.'

'You got over-excited, Daddy?' I say, following him off the bike.

'I guess your mood rubbed off on me,' he replies. He looks gorgeous tonight. His short hair is spiky and his eyes twinkle in the streetlights. The scar on his face looks like a war-trophy, won in the battle for a better life.

'I hope that's not the only part of me that's gonna rub off on you tonight,' I say.

He looks at me, practically wicked. I feel my pussy burn with lust for him.

'We'll see,' he says. Then he grabs his key from his back pocket. 'In we go, tiny brat,' he says. 'It's cocoa time.'

CHAPTER FIFTEEN

*

It's good to be back at Dane's place. The smell brings me right back, and it makes me feel super safe, straight away. It's the leather scent that's the most unusual, and the most triggering.

'What is it about bikers and leather?' I ask.

We're in Dane's kitchen. It's a very different space from my kitchen, of course. A simple stove and a small fridge, but it's still well-organized and spotlessly clean. That's something that's surprised me about Dane. I always thought that bikers were meant to be grimy and dirty, but Dane takes intense pride in cleanliness and organization.

'Well, of course leather's tough,' he says. 'Bikers always used to wear leather in case they fell of their bikes. If you're sliding across the asphalt, you need a tough layer between you and the ground.'

I grimace. 'Have you ever fallen off your bike?'

'Nah. Not me. Know people who have.'

'Like who.'

He considers for a second. 'You know what, Ripper did.'

'Rip?' I ask. For some reason I find the idea funny. Doesn't seem like something sensible old Rip would do.

'Oh sure. When Ripper was young, he was a total hellraiser. By the time I'd met him, he'd calmed down, but he came back from the army quite an angry man. Some of his exploits are famous. He don't like to talk about it so much, but Bud'll chew your ear off, if you get him talking.'

Dane slips a pan of milk onto the stove, fires up the gas.

'Sounds like Daddies MC has helped a lot of young men,' I say.

'Yep,' he nods. 'I figure we've actually saved lives. Speaking of which

— I'm sorry that we didn't get a chance to work on your business plan today. That's on me. Didn't expect to have such pressing business. I promise we'll get working on it soon, though.'

'That's OK,' I say. 'I've been thinking about it, though. And you know what, baking those cakes quickly was useful today. Got me thinking about how fast I can bake in my home kitchen. Of course, the cakes I'd be baking would be a lot more intricately decorated than the ones we made today.'

'Of course,' he says, smiling.

'What's funny?' I ask, mirroring his smile.

'Nothing. Just like it when you get all technical.'

I laugh. 'Oh that's nothing, Daddy. Just wait till I get talking about sponge to cream ratios in commercially available gift cakes.'

He growls at me. 'Ohh baby, you're getting me all hot under the collar.' He scoops up a generous teaspoon of cocoa, and mixes it into a paste in a big mug. 'Don't get me too excited, or I'll never get this drink finished for you.'

'That might not be so bad,' I say, feeling lust wash through my body like a swelling tide.

Dane looks at his watch. 'It's twenty past ten, baby. Bedtime in ten minutes. We're gonna need to get you tucked in soon. No time for funny business.'

'Aw, please?' I say, stretching my arms out across the table. I clasp my hands together, as though I'm praying. 'Just a little bit later. So we can do naughty stuff.' I'm aware that I'm pushing my luck now, and I know that Dane already owes me a spanking.

Truth is, I don't care. I've been thinking about his hands on my body all day long, dreaming about taking things further with him. I've even been fantasizing about how it might feel to have him spank me, to

CHAPTER FIFTEEN

have him tie me up.

I've been thinking all about funishments, ever since Hawk mentioned them. I wonder what I'd have to do to earn one.

'I've been thinking about you a lot today,' he says. He pours the hot, frothy milk into the mug, starts to gently stir it. 'Been thinking about your rebellious behavior. Your tendency to naughtiness.'

He lifts the spoon to his lips, blows on it, tastes the cocoa.

'Not too hot,' he says. 'That's good. Because I've also been thinking about the best way for you to experience this cocoa.'

'What do you mean?' I ask.

His eyes narrow. His voice, when he speaks, is deadly serious. 'Harper, we're gonna do a little trust exercise.'

My heart pounds. A trust exercise? 'What do you mean?' I ask.

'I'm gonna take you into the bedroom, and you're gonna put on a blindfold. Then, you have to trust me. And do whatever I ask. Do you think you can do that?'

I bite my lip. I can feel my nerves fizzing away. 'I think I can, Daddy. Nothing bad's gonna happen, is it?'

'I promise,' he says. 'Nothing bad's gonna happen. I want to show you that you can trust me. That if I ask you to do something, there's always a reason for it.'

I nod. 'OK. I'm ready.'

He takes my hand, and we head into the bedroom. I'm trembling as he sits me down on the bed.

'Are you ready to give in to trust, Harper?'

'I think so.'

'Good. You'll enjoy it, I promise.'

He opens up the drawer under his bedside table and pulls out a dark black mask.

'I'm a bit surprise you've got a blindfold,' I say, my voice trembling with anticipation.

'Sleep mask,' he says. 'Unwanted Christmas gift.' He grins. 'OK. it's going on.'

He lifts it to my eyes, and pulls it tight behind my head. Everything goes dark.

'I'm gonna lie you down now, OK?' he says.

'You can do whatever you want to me,' I whisper. I'm tingling all over. He touches my arm, and gently guides me down onto the bed.

'Now, I'm gonna take your clothes off.'

I squirm. I kinda guessed this was coming. I feel so nervous about him seeing me naked, about not being able to position myself in certain ways to accentuate the way I look. I feel so vulnerable, but it's an insane turn-on. He's gonna see me the way I really am. No filters, no nonsense.

I feel his fingers at my waist. He unbuttons my pants and I flinch.

'You OK?' he asks.

'Mmmhmm,' I reply.

His fingers go back to work, and within seconds, my pants are off. I feel the cool air against my skin. My whole body's on fire. He lifts up my top first, the fabric grazing my stomach, the bumps of my breasts. I can't help but shiver as he takes it off over my head.

I wonder what his face is like as he's looking at me. Which part of my body he's staring at. Is he looking at my breasts, hidden by my bra? Or is it my pale, smooth legs, trembling on his bed.

'Are you ready, sweetheart?' he asks

'Please,' I say, biting my lip, 'I'm ready.'

The next thing that I feel is a sharp, burning sensation on my thigh. I yelp as the sensation bites, but in mere seconds, the mild pain has gone, and it's replaced by a pleasant little tingle.

CHAPTER FIFTEEN

'That's one of my rules.' Dane's voice is close to my ear. It's low and grounded, and riciculously sexy. As he talks, his voice tracks down my body, until he's talking right next to my pussy, and I can feel the warmth of his breath on my sex. 'It hurts a bit. But only for a second. And if you can take the heat...'

He licks my thigh, swallowing up the fast-cooling liquid he spilled on me. I sigh with the pleasure of his touch. He kisses my skin now, slow, tender, soothing.

'Then you get the treat,' he says. 'So, can you take it?'

'I think so,' I say.

A moment later, another mild burning sensation — this time on my stomach. Almost instantly after, I feel Dane's lips covering the pain with pleasure. Next my shoulder, my clavicle, then, inches from my breast.

The sensation is overwhelming, and I feel lost in it. Feeling the burn and the relief is driving me wild.

'You've been very good,' he says. 'Now it's time for the reward.'

I feel him scoop me up, propping me against the headboard. He pulls the covers around me, then, a moment later, something against my lips. The smell of chocolate, the sweet taste of the cocoa. I swallow and then he lifts up the blindfold.

There he is, my Daddy, looking me in the eye. There's a hunger in his expression, a tenderness.

'Thank you for doing that with me,' he says.

'I loved it,' I say, taking another sip of my cocoa.

'Best thing is,' he says, 'we finished in time for bed. And if you can take the heat of going to bed on time, I promise that there'll be a big treat waiting for you in the future.'

'OK Daddy, you know best.'

'I... think you're wonderful, Harper.'

I can't help but blush.

'Thank you,' I say. 'Now's the time that I'd normally say that you're wrong. But you know what, I'm not putting myself down any more.'

'Good girl,' he says, kissing my forehead. 'Finish up your cocoa, and we'll do your affirmations. Then, it's snuggle time. And because you've been so good today, I'm gonna tell you a little story before bed.'

'You spoil me, Daddy,' I say.

'This is nothing,' he replies.

CHAPTER SIXTEEN

DANE

I'm telling you, I've got the bluest fucking balls in LA. No, scratch that — the bluest fucking balls in the whole country.

Last night was the biggest test of my willpower in my whole life. I had Harper — the sexiest, most outrageously fuckable woman I've ever met, in my bed, practically naked, practically begging me to ravish her. And what did I do? I poured a little hot cocoa on her trembling body, and read her a story until she fell asleep.

This Daddy game is hard. No joke. I've got a responsibility of care now. I've got to make sure I don't break my own rules, to help Harper with the things she wants to achieve in life.

And that's all fine, in theory. But this morning, I won't help me with this insane hard-on I've got. I had to turn away from cuddling Harper so that I don't wake her up with this damn iron I've got in my pants.

I didn't get much sleep through the night. Honestly, I've been in a state of fucking arousal for around three hours. It got so bad that I considered going to the bathroom and rubbing one out. I didn't want to wake her up.

So I've been sitting here in agony, desperately hoping that my boner fucking magically vanishes.

I hear a soft sound. Is that Harper? Is she awake?

I look back over my shoulder, and I see her moving. Just a tiny bit, but there's no way that she can be asleep — the movement's too coordinated.

I'm about to say good morning, but something holds me back. I'm curious, I wanna see what she's up to.

There's a little snuffle of sound from her mouth. Was that a tiny little moan?

The sound comes again, and then, to my surprise, I feel her push up against me. She's pushing her crotch — her pussy right into my ass. Fuck — is she touching herself?

Another moan, a gasp of pleasure, and now, I can feel her hand down her pants, against my back. She's moving it back and forth, up and down.

Jesus fucking Christ this is not helping me feel less horny. My cock's throbbing in my pants now, hard and heavy and desperate for some relief. I can't help myself — I move my hand down, gently stroke my manhood. I move as slow as I can — I don't want Harper to know what I'm doing.

She's moaning more, clearly trying to keep her voice down, but failing. I grip the shaft of my cock, and start to slowly pump it. This is such a bad idea. Fuck.

'Daddy,' Harper whispers, under her breath. 'Daddy...' I don't know if she's trying to get my attention, or just trying to see if I'm still asleep. But hearing her throaty voice as she whispers is driving me crazy. I need to take control of this situation, and I need to do it now.

'I know what you're doing,' I growl, keeping my voice low and even.

Harper stops still. Totally still. Then, a second later, she lets out a terrible fake snore.

I stop myself from laughing.

'You don't think I'm gonna buy that, do you?' I growl. 'When I've been listening to you moaning and groaning back there. I know what's going on. My naughty Little is indulging in some self-love in the morning.'

CHAPTER SIXTEEN

'I couldn't help myself,' she says, her voice low, almost breathless. 'After last night. After lying next to you all night. My pussy's going crazy.'

'That's cussing, sweetheart.' I'm still holding my cock, still straining lightly against my hand.

'What, pussy?' she says again. She's doing it on purpose. To test me.

'You know pussy's a naughty word. Shouldn't say it again.'

'What about cock?' she says. She grinds her crotch into my ass harder. 'Is cock a naughty word?'

'You know what?' I say. 'I feel like there should be a special punishment for breaking rules on purpose, don't you?'

I turn around to face her quickly.

She yelps with surprise. Her face is pink and glowing with effort.

'I don't want to get punished,' she says. Then she gives me an evil look. 'Just for saying pussy.'

'You're still touching yourself, aren't you?' I say. 'You're still rubbing that hot little pussy, still pushing your fingers up the slick passage.'

She bites her lip, and moves her arm again.

'I can't stop,' she says. 'Looking at your face. Thinking about your lips on my body last night. Imagining what your hands might feel like on my body.'

'You're gonna find out exactly what they feel like on your body,' I say. 'Because I'm about to spank your ass. Hard. One for each cuss word. I've been counting, young lady. You've got five spanks coming your way. And until I'm finished, you're not gonna touch yourself. You understand me?'

'Yes Daddy,' she says. Her breathing's deep with pleasure, her eyes glazed over with lust.

I pull myself away, get out of bed.

She looks at me, then, looks down to my boxer shirts. Her eyes nearly pop out of her head.

'Daddy!' she says. 'You're... you're excited.'

I look down. My cock's so thick, so big, that it's poking out the top of my shorts.

'That's none of your concern young lady,' I say. I sit down on the edge of the bed. My cock's sticking straight up into the air. I'm going berserk, desperate to touch it, desperate to bury it in Harper's tiny, pink pussy.

'Come lie on my lap,' I grunt.

'Oh f-' she starts. 'I mean. If I do that, your... thing will touch me.'

'You just have to deal with it.' I say.

'But it's gonna make me so wet,' she whines. 'I'm gonna be soaking through my panties. It's gonna go all over your... thing.'

'I can deal with it,' I say.

I don't know if I *can* deal with it.

She doesn't exactly get out of bed. No. She wriggles her way over to me. It's exactly like she's a naughty kid, trying to avoid punishment. Well, it's not gonna work on me.

When she's close enough, I grab her. She whoops as I pull her across my knee.

'I didn't think I'd have to be disciplining you so soon after last night,' I say.

'Sorry I disappointed you, Daddy,' she says. But it doesn't sound like she means it.

'Of course you are,' I say. I grab the waist of her pants, and tug them down. She gasps with surprise.

Fuck. She *is* wet. I can see her panties, totally sodden all around the

CHAPTER SIXTEEN

crotch. My cock's prodding up, edging into her, so close to her sweet, tight entrance.

'I'm gonna have to tug your panties down now, Harper.'

'Hnngggg,' she groans. Her hands slip back, grab her panties, and she tries to tug them down herself.

'No,' I say, swatting them gently away. 'I'm in charge here. We do this on my time-frame.'

She huffs. 'But I'm so horrrrnnny,' she says.

'I'm sorry, that's gonna have to wait.'

I slowly — as slowly as I can manage — pull her pink cotton panties down her thighs. They bunch and twist until the fabric is tightly wound. Looks like it could snap at any second. Just like me.

Her ass is fucking perfect — and I mean absolutely damn flawless. All that bike riding has left her body toned and supple, like a young peach. I let my hand rest on her firm, soft flesh, and she whimpers beneath me. I feel a gush of liquid, as pussy spit dangles onto the tip of my cock.

'Oh f- dang,' she says, her words shuddering from her over-excited mouth like quivering moths.

I gently part the cheeks of her ass, look at her sweet rosebud, feast my eyes on the slice of hot pink between her legs. Her pussy is fucking beautiful — so wet and plump and fuckable. Just thinking about how it would feel wrapped around my cock is driving me crazy.

'When I spank you, I want you to say sorry for cussing, Harper. It's the only way you'll learn.'

'Yes Daddy,' she whispers. She's shifting around in my lap, trying to rub her pussy on the tip of my cock, trying to reach for me.

I bring my hand up, then slap it down with a smack. She cries out in surprise, then moans with pleasure as the pain gives way to something else.

'What do you say?' I ask.

'Sorry, Daddy. Sorry for cussing.'

With each smack, she shivers more, and her pussy gets wetter and wetter. My cock's straining upwards, desperate for a kiss of those pouty lips. But this isn't the time — I still need to take things slow. But that doesn't mean I can't give her a taste, give her some relief from this torture.

After the fifth and final smack, she lets out a long, low moan, ending with a, 'Nnnngsorry Daddy. I won't do it again. I promise.'

'Good,' I say.

'Please,' she says. 'I'm desperate for you, my private parts are going nuts. If you don't touch me, I'm gonna explode.'

'Explode, huh?' I ask. 'Sounds dangerous.' I start to walk my fingers up the back of her legs, skipping them across her peach-smooth skin.

'Mmmhm, I've heard of it. Girls who were so horny that their froo-froos exploded.'

'That's not what I want,' I say. 'Because I kinda like the woman that this froo-froo is attached to.'

I run the tips of my fingers lightly across her pussy lips. Up and down slowly, feeling the delicate folds of her opening. It's like a soft flower. I gently push the petals apart. She twitches in my grip, as her breathing speeds up. She pushes back, trying to force my fingers inside her, but I hold back.

'I want you to want me more than you've ever wanted anything,' I say.

'I do,' she pants.

'More than cake,' I say.

'I'll never eat cake again,' she pants, 'if I can just feel your fingers

CHAPTER SIXTEEN

inside me.'

I push them in. One at first, then, a moment later, the second. Slow but firm, knuckle-deep, and then I gently push further.

'That's it,' she says.

'You're mine, Harper, you belong to me.'

'I do,' she says. I slowly draw my fingers back, and she quivers with every inch. I pull them all the way back, then rub them over her rigid clit, making her moan as I gently grip, before pulling them back, and ramming them back into her.

'You're gonna take whatever I give you, aren't you?' I grunt, leaning in, kissing her back.

'I'm gonna take all of you,' she says. 'I need you.'

I fuck her faster with my fingers, beckoning back inside her, making her squirm. She wriggles and writhes, but I hold her down, letting her know that when she's with me, I'm calling the shots.

'I like that,' she says, 'I love the way you hold me. I love the way your fingers feel.'

I move my thumb over her clit as I keep thrusting in and out of her, and then, just as I feel like she's about to cum, I grab her body and slip her off me. I flip her over, and I push my face into her pussy, ramming my tongue in deep, tasting the honeyed sweetness of her juice, lapping her up.

She screams, yells, reaches down to grab my hair, and then, seconds later, her body starts to buck and tense, as she surrenders to my assault, and to her pleasure.

'Oh Daddy,' she sighs, when she's finally still. 'That was-'

'Fucking perfect,' I finish.

'Effing perfect,' she echoes, laughing beautifully.

CHAPTER SEVENTEEN

HARPER

'I'm gonna need a calculator.' Dane's sitting across from me, looking at a sheet of paper covered with my hastily scratched-out ideas.

'Use your phone!' I say.

'Phones have calculators on them?' he asks, raising an eyebrow.

'OK, boomer,' I say.

He gives me a blank look. 'Did you just forget my name? How do you know Boomer?'

I can't help but smile. 'Is there honestly someone called Boomer in Daddies MC?'

He nods. 'I'm so lost right now, Harper.'

I reach across the table and give him a kiss on the head. 'You're in LA, with your gorgeous Little, Harper, and you're helping her with her very big, very clever, very grown-up business plan.'

'Aha!' he says, pretending to finally understand something. 'Everything suddenly makes sense. Thank fuck for that.' He takes out his phone and commands it. 'Phone, open the calculator.'

I burst out into laughter.

'Got you,' he says, giving me a mischievous grin. 'I know how to use my damn phone.' He holds up my sheet of paper. 'Damn, I didn't know butter was actually that expensive.'

After Dane gave me the best dang orgasm of my life, he decided to give me another gift. We're going over the beginnings of my business plan. If only I could think of a good name for my bakery. So far, the best I've come up with is Harper's Cakes.

I know. It's terrible.

My mind keeps flicking back to what Dane did to me this morning. The masterful way that he spanked me. The way he held me still while his fingers explored my pussy. And then, the incredible, animistic way he threw me down and pushed his tongue up inside me.

For like, half an hour, my legs were shaking afterward. Even though a couple hours have gone by, I still feel like I'm tingling.

The terrible thing is, I'm still horny as all hell! I keep glancing down at Dane's crotch, thinking about what he's got hiding down there. I saw how big and thick it was. Just thinking about his cock now is making my mouth water.

What with that and all this cake chat, I'm a dribbling wreck.

I hope that Dane wants to have sex with me. I mean, I know that he was hard as hell this morning, but we still didn't get down and dirty. I'm grateful to him for taking things slow with me — it's been wonderful getting to know him before doing anything sexual — but I feel like I actually am gonna burst if we don't take things to the next level soon.

I'm starting to think that there's something wrong with me. That he's gone off me or something. It's just my insecurity talking, right?

'Have you thought about having a gimmick?' Dane muses. 'Like specializing in kid's cakes or something? I feel like that jerk, Frank, has cornered the celebrity cake market. But you really understand cute.'

He's standing up now, walking around the table, holding my 'business plan' in front of him. I get the feeling that he does his best thinking while on his feet.

'Hey, that's a good idea,' I say.

'Wouldn't it be great if you could go public about being a Little. Advertise yourself as being a world expert in making the cutest cakes known to man?'

'I don't think people would get it,' I say, suddenly full of terror and

CHAPTER SEVENTEEN

apprehension. What would happen if I *did* come out as a Little. What would Felicity say? What would Frank and Blake say?

'You might be right. Might not work as a business strategy. But it might be good for your self-confidence. Tell your friends. I don't know though, I'm not an expert.'

'I don't know,' I say, eager to change the subject.

'Hey, no pressure darling. I was just thinking aloud.'

'It's OK, Daddy. I like that you're so confident. So sure of who you are and who I am.'

He smiles.

'You know what? This is a very, very good start. You've gone into a lot of detail here. All these flour and sugar sums are very impressive.' He scratches his head. 'Math was never my strong suit.'

'Really?' I say. 'Nerdy guy like you?'

'Oh, if the guys knew what I let you get away with,' he grins. 'Until that smart-ass comment, I was gonna say how impressed I've been with your work today. Great affirmations this morning, and then your business plan.'

'You can still say you're impressed,' I say. Pudding's sitting next to me at the table. I grab him and give him a cuddle, then I hold him up to my ear. 'Pudding says that he thinks I've been a good girl.'

'Pudding, you're right. I'll admit it. I'm super proud of you, pumpkin.' He walks over and leans down, kisses the top of my head. 'How do you feel?'

'Good,' I say. 'Worried that even though I'm making this business plan, it might all come to nothing.'

'Hey, if you don't make it, it'll definitely come to nothing,' he says.

'I guess that's true.'

'Don't worry. It'll be worth your while, I promise. Now, don't get too excited, but I've got something for us to do. Well, mainly for you to do. A little reward for doing all your chores for the day.'

'A treat?!' I shriek with excitement.

'A treat. It's nothing too exciting, so don't get too hyped up.'

'Too late!' I say, clapping my hands together. I wonder what kind of activity Daddy's got planned. 'Ooh ooh this is too cool!'

'Well,' he says, looking slightly sheepish, 'I asked around at the club, trying to get some ideas of stuff you might want to do, and the guys were basically unanimous. Just wait here for a second, I'll be back.'

I sit at the table for what seems like an eternity, but is most likely about twenty seconds. When Dane returns, he's got a bag with him.

'I feel like the guys are putting me up to this,' he says, shaking his head. 'But I kept asking them, and they kept telling me. She'll love it, they said.'

'Why?' she asks, 'What have you got.'

'We're playing makeup,' he says.

'Makeup?' I say, confused.

'Yep.' He empties the bag on the table, and tons of different cosmetic products fly out, spinning across the table. Mascara, foundation, lipstick, blusher, eyeliner, every type of product you can possibly imagine. There's so much of it here, in so many different shades and colors.

My eyes widen. 'There's so much!'

'I didn't know what to get. I just let the woman in the store help me.' He's looking at the mess of products on the table, shaking his head. 'This is nuts.'

'So, you just bought this for me? I'm gonna put makeup on myself? Do you have a mirror?'

He looks at me. 'That's not the game,' he says. 'I'm gonna try to do

CHAPTER SEVENTEEN

yours.' He pauses, rolls his eyes. 'And then you're gonna do mine.'

My eyes widen, my mouth falls open.

'You don't want to do it, I can tell,' he says.

'Ooohhhhhhhh my Daddy, you couldn't be more wrong. Let me at it!'

*

You know what? Having Dane put makeup on me is one of the most strangely intimate, erotic experiences of my life. How often do you have someone that close to you? Staring into your eyes? Brushing things softly over your face?

He's just inches away from me, looking at my face with the eye of a craftsman. It's almost like he's painting me, and I guess in a way, he is.

I thought this was gonna be fun — and it is — but this extra layer of closeness is making it a wonderful bonding activity.

'No-one's ever done my makeup before. Well, not like this.'

'I hope you like it,' he says. He looks at a couple sticks of lipstick, trying to choose between a deep red and a pale pink.

Choose the pink, Dane, choose the pink!

He grabs the red and moves it towards my lips. I bite my tongue. I'd never normally choose a shade like this, but that's kinda why this is so much fun.

'How on earth do you get it neat?' Dane says, as he carefully, slowly applies the lipstick. It's a thrill to have him push the waxy stick into my lips. I can tell this is the first time he's ever done this, but even so, he's not being shy. He's trying everything out.

'Practice,' I say, when he finishes. I smack my lips together. 'That look any better?'

'Yeah,' he says. 'Good trick.'

'Oh the things men don't know,' I giggle.

'Seems like I know a thing or two.'

'Oh, you definitely do.'

'Wanna see how you look?' he asks. There's a hint of nerves in his voice, but only a hint.

'You bet I do!' I say.

'OK. Promise not to hate me.' He passes me a small hand mirror.

'Oh my...' I say. 'I look like... I don't know.' I start to laugh. 'Hehe, Daddy, subtlety isn't your strong suit, is it?'

I've never had so much makeup on in my life. I actually do kinda look like an oil painting. A thick layer of foundation, way too much blusher, what look like bags under my eyes thanks to eye shadow, and bright red lips, that are so big that it looks as they've been painted on.

I snort with laughter, bring my hand to my mouth.

'I thought I did a pretty good job.' He tries to keep a straight face, but within seconds, he's chuckling too. 'My inspiration was,' he snorts with laughter, 'a sexy clown.'

I let out a huge, very unwomanly laugh, I can feel tears in my eyes. 'Oh no!' I shriek, 'I'm gonna ruin my beautiful makeup!'

He howls with laughter, doubling over, and wipes his own eyes. 'Holy shit this it too fucking funny. Damn. You're gonna get your own back on me, aren't you?'

I nod. 'You bet your butt I will.' All of a sudden, a naughty idea pops into my head. 'You know what though? I'm gonna need you to sit over there, away from the table. Need to get close to you.'

'OK,' he says, a little suspicious, but he does what I ask, moving his chair away from the table.

'Now, I'm gonna assume the position that a professional makeup

CHAPTER SEVENTEEN

artist would take,' I say. I walk up to him, taking a lipstick along with me, and then, before he has a chance to say anything, I hop onto his lap, straddling him, a leg on either side.

'Professional makeup artist?' he says. He's so close to me, I feel his breath on my neck.

'Mmhmm,' I say, grinding my pussy down into him just a little. 'Very professional.'

'Seems that way,' he says. I feel his cock harden beneath me, pushing up into my sex. Damn he's big. Damn, he's *hard*.

'Now I'm gonna apply lipstick to you, the way a professional would.' I take the lipstick, and paint it onto my lips. Then, I lean in close, and kiss Dane carefully on his lips. At first, I try to be careful, as though I really am trying to apply makeup.

But within seconds, I'm lost in him, pushing my body up against him, my hands encircling him, the makeup forgotten. He's holding me, too, running his hands up and down my back, squeezing my ass as his tongue dips into my mouth.

'I want you,' he groans.

'I want you too,' I whisper back, eyes closed, lips next to his ear.

'I'm gonna fuck you while you're in that makeup, Harper.'

I open my eyes to see him grinning at me.

'If that's what you like, I'm never gonna change it again,' I laugh.

'I don't care what your fucking makeup looks like. I don't care if you don't wear any. All I care about, is that I'm with you, and you're with me.'

He surges up from the chair, lifting me as easily as if I weigh nothing, then he pushes me up against the wall, exploring my body with his hands, tearing at my top. Suddenly, he pushes his fingers in my mouth.

'Bite em,' he growls.

I do as he asks.

'Harder babygirl.'

As I bit down harder he tugs at my pants, and they fall to the floor. And then, just as he thrusts his hands down my panties, I hear something.

'Is that a land line phone?' I ask, in disbelief.

'God fucking damn it!' he growls. 'It's the Daddies MC phone. I've gotta fucking take it.'

My heart's beating so hard I swear I can hear it over the phone.

'Can't you leave it? I'm all wet and bothered.'

He groans. 'Honey, no-one uses that phone line unless it's a matter of life and death.'

Life and death. I guess that's important. I guess.

'I'm sorry,' he continues, as he puts me down on the ground. 'Wish I didn't have to stop. Trust me, I don't want to be doing anything but this right now.'

I see his cock, pushing against his jeans. 'Ugh! I'm gonna pass out!' I whine.

'You'll be fine. I'll be back in a minute.'

He runs into the other room, and grabs the phone.

'This is Dane,' I hear, and then, I don't catch anything much of what he says. I pull my pants back on, try not to feel like I've just been rejected.

A few minutes later, he returns to the room, a serious look on his face.

'What's up?' I say, trying to hide the disappointment in my voice.

'That was Ripper. We've got the location. Old place in the heart of the Fashion District.'

CHAPTER SEVENTEEN

'So, what's the plan?' I say.

'The plan can wait.' He says. 'Right now, I've got to get a fuckin' tattoo.'

CHAPTER EIGHTEEN

DANE

'This place doesn't exactly look... reputable.'

Harper's behind me on my hog, holding me close. How I wish I was back at my place with her right now, instead of getting ready to apologize to Rock. Ugh.

The apology's gonna hurt more than the fucking tat.

But for what's going to go down, especially as Bud's providing back-up, I need Rock. Because even though he and I get on about as well as Batman and Joker, I know that I can trust him. More than any other member, Rock's loyalty to Daddies MC is unshakable.

'It's not reputable,' I reply. 'That's kinda the point. Rock only works with clients that he picks.'

Harper hops off the bike. 'He chooses his clients?'

'Uh-huh. Doesn't want people walking in off the streets.'

'How does he make any money?' she asks.

'Well,' I say begrudgingly, 'the guy's a fucking genius. That's got something to do with it. He's got a waiting list as long as-'

'Your thing?'

I shake my head. 'Damn, Harper, you've got a one-track mind.'

'Not normally,' she says, blushing, 'but you got me all riled-up and now I'm all... you know.'

'I know sugar, and I promise, we're gonna take care of that just as soon as we can.' I lean into her and pull her in close. 'I'm gonna make you come so hard you forget your fucking name.'

'Yes please,' she breathes.

'First though,' I say, 'I need to eat some humble pie.'

LUCKY MOON

It's a dark, dirty doorway, in a grimy alley with no streetlights. Above the door, in purple neon, is a sign that simply reads: Rock 'N' Roll Tattoo.

'I've been putting this off for far too long,' I say, sighing deep. 'Been waiting for Rock to come apologize to me. But that's not gonna happen. So... here we are.'

I knock on the door, and wait a few seconds. 'Who's that?' It's Lisa, Rock's current squeeze. Rock has more fucking girlfriend's than I've had hot dinners, and he always gets them to work the front desk of his tattoo parlor. He's cheap like that.

'Dane. Here to see Rock.'

'Dane? You serious?'

'Just tell him I'm here, Lisa.'

'Who's that?' Harper asks, as Lisa goes in to get Rock.

'His Little,' I say. 'Not normally one to judge but, uh, Lisa can be a little... fiery. Rock's a complicated guy, and he tends to attract interesting women.'

'At least she's not a member of the Blood Fuckers,' says Harper.

'Hey!'

'That doesn't count! That's the name of their gang. How else am I mean to say it?'

'Fine, I'll let you off, but next time you say the f-word, you won't be able to sit down for a couple days.'

'What do you... ohhhh, a spanked bum.' She giggles. 'That would be terrible.'

Before I have a chance to reply, the door swings open.

'Well look what the cat finally fucking dragged in.'

Rock looks good, damn him. He's a lean guy, in his mid-thirties, but his scraggy beard makes him look a little older. He's got long, jet-black

CHAPTER EIGHTEEN

hair and chiseled cheekbones, and the kind of intense, blue eyes that make girls swoon. He's chewing a toothpick right now in an attempt to finally quit smoking, and he plays with it between his teeth, rolling and flicking it.

'Good to see you, Rock.'

'Shame I can't say the same, hog-wrecker.' He looks over at Harper. 'Damn, who's this tasty lil' biscuit?' His eyes run up and down her pale arms. 'Virgin skin, too. You come here to get some ink, Baby?'

'No she has not,' I say, keeping my voice even and cool. 'I thought you had a two year waiting list?'

'I make exceptions for virgin skin, Dane, you know that.'

'Does it hurt?' Harper says.

'Course it hurts,' I growl. 'Hurts like hell.'

'It's good pain, though,' Rock purrs. 'You're in control, or at least, I will be. You tell me to stop, I stop. You tell me to go?' He takes the toothpick outta his mouth and flashes a smile, his one golden tooth twinkles in the light. 'I go.'

I'm not taking this. 'Rock, so help me, I came here to apologize to you, but you're walking on thin ice, brother. Harper is mine. My Little. No fucking sharing. No sleazy remarks. You keep your hands to yourself, and to your clients, you understand?'

Harper looks up at me. Is that respect in her eyes, or anger?

Rock holds his hands up. 'I get it. You've claimed her. She's yours. No problem. Now did you say something about an apology?'

I sigh.

'Rock, I need a favor.'

'That don't sound like an apology.' He crosses his arms. 'I was hoping this could be a fresh start for us.'

'I'm gonna apologize.' I say. 'I just need you to know that I've got an ulterior motive. Gonna be honest with you up-front. It's the only way I know how to be.'

He considers this. 'Go on,' he eventually nods.

'You were at the vote, weren't you? The vote about trying to stop the drug-dealing in our turf.'

'Yeah,' he says. 'Unlike some people here, I could be bothered to show up.'

'Don't push it,' I growl. 'I had my reasons for missing that vote. Anyway, look, here's the deal.'

I explain the situation with the Blood Fuckers, the way they've been smuggling drugs in cake boxes into our turf, and the implications.

'If we let them get too big, garner too much influence, they'll start to make things difficult for us. You know that want us out of LA. '

He nods. 'Ever since we stopped that deal a couple years ago, they've been gunning for our blood.'

It's true. Hawk and I disrupted a heroin deal that cost the Blood Fuckers nearly a hundred grand, and they were furious. Since then, they've been attacking our club members. Titus got nearly killed, attacked by two of the BF just two blocks from The Milk Shed. And if they get bigger, the beatings will only get worse.

'So, Hawk, Ripper and I decided that we've got to put a stop to this new influx of drugs. Not only that,' I look up and down the alley, just to make sure there's no-one around. 'We're going after Satan.'

He nods, considers what I've just said. 'What do you need,' he says.

'I need you to help me raid their headquarters.'

He lifts his eyebrows. 'Fuck, you know where their HQ is?'

'Yep. Got good intel.'

'Well,' he says, drawing in breath between our teeth, 'you know I'm gonna help, don't you?'

CHAPTER EIGHTEEN

Fuck. Thank God. For all his bluster, Rock really *is* one of the toughest dudes I know. Before his career as a tattoo artist really took off, he was a bare-knuckle fighter. There's no-one I'd rather have at my side than Rock.

'Good,' I say.

'Haven't finished,' he says, flashing a grin. 'There's only one thing I need.'

'Don't make me,' I say, shaking my head.

'Come on,' he prods. 'It won't hurt.'

'Fine. I'm sorry. I'm sorry that I made you scratch your damn bike.'

Harper looks up at me, incredulous. '*That's* the terrible thing that's ruined your friendship?'

'It's complicated!' I say.

'It's not complicated,' Rock says, between snorts of laughter, 'just fucking expensive. I just got a custom paint-job on my Heritage Softail Classic. Hawk did it for me — guy's a miracle-worker, but his prices aren't miraculous.'

'Sometimes you bikers are more like squabbling brothers than hardcore badboys,' says Harper.

'You take that back,' Rock says, fake-angry.

'How did you scratch it?' Harper says.

'I was drunk.' I say. 'As a very fucking drunk skunk.'

'So it *was* your fault?' She says.

'No!' I reply, 'He drove into my bike. On purpose. Because we had an argument.'

'I was drunk, too,' Rock admits. 'Maybe even drunker than a fucking drunk skunk.'

Harper rolls her eyes. 'What were you arguing about?'

'Don't remember,' we both say at the same time.

'Sounds like you two need Daddies,' Harper says. 'Or maybe Little Harper could be your mommy?' She says, hands on hips. She puts on a silly, deep voice, 'If you two boys don't stop fighting, I'm gonna spank your little bot-bots!'

Rock laughs. 'Damn Dane, you've got a live-wire here. Congrats you two.'

'Thanks,' I reply. 'So, can I count on you for the raid?'

'Oh,' he says, 'you think I needed an apology?'

'What?' I say, my eyes narrowing. 'That's what you said.'

'Nope.' He smiles a shit-eating grin. 'Just said I needed something.'

'Fuc-'

'Daddy,' Harper says, grabbing my arm. 'Let's play nice.'

Damn. She's right. 'Well Rock, as my Babygirl has reminded me, it's nice to be nice. What is it that you need?'

'You made a mark on my bike. So, I need to make a mark on you. You get a tattoo, right here, right now.'

'What of?' I ask.

He thinks it over.

'You know what, your Little seems a sensible girl. Why don't we let her choose?'

I look at Harper. She looks at me.

'I don't know,' she says. 'Seems like a bad idea. Why don't you choose, Rock?'

'No.' I hold up my hand. 'Harper, I trust you — much more than I trust this fucking reprobate. You can choose.'

'Good!' says Rock, clapping his hands together. 'I think you've got a little real estate on your arm still, haven't you?'

I nod, angrily. I can't believe I'm having to do this. Poor Harper, under all this pressure. I hope she chooses something OK. Fuck. Why

CHAPTER EIGHTEEN

did I ever think that coming to apologize to Rock would be a good idea?

'So, Babygirl, what do you think. You got an idea?'

Harper nods.

'Well, come whisper it to me. Don't want Dane to see it 'til it's finished.'

My Little Girl looks at me, then walks over to Rock, and whispers in his ear. His eyes widen, and he chuckles.

'Oooh boy,' he says. 'This is gonna be fun!'

CHAPTER NINETEEN

HARPER

Dane winces as he shifts off Angeline, and then again as he unlocks his front door.

'Does it hurt, Daddy?' I ask, stroking his other arms.

'It's a bit sore. Nothing I can't deal with.'

He pushes the door open and I follow him in. He's been strangely quiet ever since we got into the tattoo studio, and Rock started to get to work on him. I hope he's not too upset. It must be horrible to have something you didn't choose tattooed on you.

'I hope you're not mad.' I blurt out, as I kick off my shoes.

'Hey, it was my decision to have you choose the design. You were put on the spot, sugar. Not expecting amazing new ink, just better than the crap Rock would have chosen.'

Watching Dane get tattooed was an experience like no other. I've never been in a tattoo parlor before, and it wasn't quite like anywhere else I'd been. The buzz of the tattoo guns, the smell of the ink and the disinfectant. Then there was the actual tattooing itself. Watching Rock drag that gun across Dane's smooth skin, seeing blood and ink pool up from the surface, marveling as new black lines stayed inside his arm.

'It was kinda cool, seeing it happen,' I say.

It's getting late, but it's not bedtime just yet. I'm terrified right now at the thought that Dane's gonna flip out when he sees what I chose for him. Why didn't I go for something that he'd like? Something like... I don't know, the Harley Davidson symbol, or a gun, or something else tough and rough.

Instead, I head to pick something dumb. Something *meaningful*.

He's gonna hate it, I just know.

'Didn't feel so cool,' he grunts.

'I can imagine.'

'You honestly never thought about getting any ink?' he asks me.

'No way. Needles are super scary. Plus, I'm so flighty, I'd get something that I'd end up regretting like, two weeks later.'

Dane's new artwork is safely hidden under layers of cling-film right now, and he's still wearing his jacket. But it's only a matter of time.

'I should probably clean it,' Dane finally says. 'You wanna come watch? I'm gonna give you a bath straight after.'

'A bath? Do you think I need one, Daddy?'

'Absolutely you need one, young lady. You've been on the bike, through traffic. Probably all sorts of oil and muck on you.'

I nod. My heart starts to race. He's gonna see his tattoo, any second.

I follow Dane into the bathroom. He mulls something over. 'You know what, I'm gonna give you a bath first. My tattoo can wait a minute. Wanna live in blissful ignorance a little while longer.' He leans over and yanks the taps, and in moments, hot water is flooding the tub. 'Got this for you the other day,' he says, grabbing a container of bubble bath. 'How bubbly you like it?'

'Really bubbly,' I say.

'I shoulda known,' he says.

'Um, can you come in the bath with me?' I say, wringing my hands together behind my back.

'You trying to give me an infection?' He shakes his head. 'I can't use any products on this. A tattoo at this stage is an open wound, sweetheart. Only thing that goes on this bad boy is warm water and cling film. Some baby cream to keep it moist.'

'You're gonna use baby cream?' I grin.

CHAPTER NINETEEN

'Watch that lip,' he says. 'Or I'll cover your butt with this cream and put you in a diaper.' He pauses a second when he sees my expression, then he realizes what he's said. 'Damn, Babygirl, I'm sorry. Didn't mean to bring back bad memories.' He grabs his hair, shakes his head. 'I can be fucking stupid when I wanna be. Don't worry. No diapers for you, sugar.'

'Thank you,' I say. 'I knew you were only playing around.'

'Good,' he says. 'I'd hate to hurt your feelings, or make you scared.'

'You couldn't!' I say. 'But I'm worried about your tattoo. Should I just tell y-'

He raises his hand. 'Don't ruin the surprise. Now come on, bath's ready. Let's get you out of those clothes.'

I pull my top up and over my head, then my pants, in no time I'm standing in front of him in my bra and panties.

'Feel a bit self-conscious,' I say, trembling a little.

'Don't worry, sweetheart, I'm just wanna make sure you get nice and clean. Want me to help you with your bra and panties?'

I nod.

He circles behind me, his fingers trail up my back, leaving a line of electricity. He unhooks my bra, and it falls down to the ground. Then, he lets his hands rest on my hips for just a second, before gently pulling my panties down.

'Thanks, Daddy,' I say.

'No problem. Any chance I get to check out this perfect little ass, I'm gonna take it.'

I look back. 'Hey!'

'Just being honest. Now come on, hand on my shoulder as you step into the bath. Don't want you slipping down.'

He steps to my side, and I do as he asks. The water is perfect — so warm and full of prickly little bubbles. Moments later, I'm sitting in the bath with my legs crossed and the water up to the lower edge of my breasts.

'How's the water.'

'Great!' I say.

'Now don't splash me,' he says. 'I know what you Littles are like.'

'Daddy! I'd never dream of it,' I grin.

'Time to get you clean.' Dane grabs a big, natural sponge from the side of the bath, before dunking it in the tub, and drawing it across my back.

I decide it's time to ask a question I've been dreading having to ask.

'So, did you and Rock choose a time for the raid?'

I'm terrified of things going wrong. Dane, Hawk, Rip and even Rock, feel like a new family for me. The thought of them getting hurt — or worse — is awful.

'Mmmhmm,' he says. He looks at me, with serious eyes. 'Tomorrow.'

My heart pounds.

'Tomorrow?'

'The sooner the better. If we coulda gone today, I woulda.'

'I just thought we might have a bit more time together.'

Dane draws the sponge across my stomach, then swiftly wipes the rough surface of the sponge across my breasts, making my nipples harden, and a bolt of pleasure shoot around my body.

'We've got all the time in the world, honey,' he says. Then, he looks puzzled. 'What you worried about?'

I stick out my lower lip. 'You know. I'm just... worried.'

'You worried something's gonna happen to me, huh?'

I nod. 'Maybe.'

CHAPTER NINETEEN

'Have faith, sweet thing. Nothing's gonna happen to me. I'm smart, and Hawk's brave, and Rock's tough. Between the three of us, we'll destroy the Blood Fuckers. Ruin their drug dealing operation. Run them out of town.'

'How?' I ask. I wait for a moment. 'Are you gonna kill them?'

He looks at me like I'm crazy. 'No, honey, we're not gonna kill them. You honestly think I'm capable of something like that?'

'I dunno.'

He's washing my shoulders now, cleaning my skin carefully, being so kind and tender. Could these be the hands of a killer?

'Honestly, I don't know myself. Never been in the position to need to find out. Never have though. I'm not violent by nature — you've probably worked that out. Having said that, if anyone ever threatened you, I don't know what I'd do. But it wouldn't be pretty.'

'Lucky I'm so safe with you, then,' I say. I reach up and touch his hand.

'I don't fucking deserve you, Harper. When I think about losing you, I just…' He trails off. I've never heard him sound like this before. Never heard him sound vulnerable. 'I never used to be scared of dying,' he finally says. Didn't care about it. Always thought that when it was my time, it would just be my time.' He rubs the sponge on one thigh, then the second. 'Now though, I do care. Because I can't deal with the thought that I might never see you again. And I don't want to think of you without me. Because I need you, and you need me.'

Then, carefully, he pushes the sponge between my legs. I gasp as he cleans my pussy, grabbing his arm, hoping he'll never stop.

'You helped me know myself,' he says. 'I'm a Daddy Dom. I'm sure of it.'

My heart's pounding. My body's on fire.

'Daddy, you should look at your tattoo.'

He gives me a confused look, then he reaches down, and pulls off his shirt. He looks at his arm, and through the cling-film, the script of the tattoo is obvious. Written in a badass gothic font are two simple words: Daddy Dom.

He meets my eyes, and for a moment, it almost looks as though he might cry. But he doesn't.

'I love it,' he says. 'The best tattoo I ever got.'

'I'm so glad,' I say, smiling wide.

'Bath-time's over,' he says. 'Get out, please.'

I bite my lip, and step out of the bath. I stand in front of him, wet, warm and naked. He looks me up and down.

'I'm gonna fuck you now, Harper. Gonna make you mine.' He steps up so that he's close. 'Unbuckle my belt.' His voice is as serious as an assault rifle.

'Yes Daddy,' I say. I tug at the thick belt, pull it apart.

'Pants down.' He orders.

I grab them, pull them down his legs. Glancing down, I see the thick, rod-like shape of his cock. Hard and upright, long and dangerous.

'Touch me,' he says, commanding. Dominant.

As I reach down to his underwear, I tremble with anticipation. I've been waiting for this moment for so long.

'I'm so wet,' I say. 'Everywhere.'

His cock feels warm and hard. I pull his boxers down, unleashing it. It springs back up, desperate for me to touch him again. I wrap my hand around it, squeeze it, feel its weight.

'I wanna feel your wetness on me,' he says. He reaches forward, and slowly moves his hand down my stomach. I shiver as he traces a line straight down to my pussy, then pushes his fingers into me. He moves

CHAPTER NINETEEN

gently, parting my lips, and I moan as he explores me. Then, as he draws out, I almost feel like I'm gonna cum, right here and now. My legs shake, but I control myself.

I watch as he paints his cock with my pussy juice, then puts his hand around mine, squeezing gently.

'That's it, baby,' he says. 'That feels fucking good.'

'You feel good,' I say. 'The way you touch me. Like you own me.'

'You belong to me. I belong to you.'

I lean into him, avoiding his tender arm, leaning on his chest. I kiss his skin, pushing my wet body on his dry, and he reaches round, cups my ass, pulls me into him. His cock presses against my belly, my wetness slipping against my flesh.

'Please Daddy, I can't wait any longer. Take me.'

He growls, gripping my arms, then he lifts me up, sits my ass on the rim of the bath. His cock's there instantly, pushing against the lips of my pussy, hot against me.

'Oh fuck,' he says, 'you're so wet.'

'Let me show you how wet I am on the inside,' I say.

'I want to fucking destroy you,' he says. 'I want to fuck you so damn hard you pass out.'

'Please,' I say.

His cock slips in and I *feel* my pussy stretch to accommodate him. My mouth widens, my eyes rolls back, my hands grip the rim of the bath so hard my knuckles go white. He pushes in further, inch by inch, training my pussy to take his monster cock, helping me cope with the pleasure slowly.

'Oh Daddy,' I say, 'Oh f-'

'Say it,' he says. 'When we're like this, you can say it.'

'Oh fuck,' I whine, my voice high-pitched, desperate. 'It feels so good.'

Then he's farther in and I'm panting, and then his balls are nestled up right next to my butt and he's so deep, deeper than any man before, so deep I feel like he's plugged into me, like we're the same person.

'So fuckin' tight,' he grunts. He bites his lip hard, grimacing. 'Fuck Harper, you're incredible.'

'I can't-' I try, 'It's so-'

And then, he moves. Slow at first. I feel every inch, every tiny bump and vein, every hard, part of him. Watching him move — the muscles of his body, the expression on his face. It's almost too much.

'Strap in, baby, because things are about to get bumpy.'

He grips me hard, lifting me, and then, he slides into me, in and out like a machine, a machine designed to give me pleasure, to make me feel loved. Because that *is* how I feel. Not just wanted, not just cared for, but fucking loved.

His hands grab my back, and he pounds into me now, making me gasp with every move. He's incredible, and he's mine, and I can't believe it.

'Daddy, more, harder, please, I can take it.'

But when he really starts to move, I don't know that I *can* take it. He's furious, enraged, growling and grunting with each thrust. Then he grabs me, twists me round, splays me out on the rug by the bath. My ass is against the cold floor and somehow, Dane's further in me, fucking me harder. One hand on my clit, the other in my mouth. I suck his fingers as he uses my body, and for a moment, I feel like his bike, as his motor makes me sing, and his soul makes me growl.

'I'm gonna, I'm gonna-'

'Cum for Daddy,' he shouts, 'Cum for me Harper, I want to feel your pussy tight round that cock.'

CHAPTER NINETEEN

He pushes me over the edge, and I yowl with the intensity of it — the ecstasy, the surprise of it. For a moment, it feels like the world is falling apart, and then, a second later, as his cock starts to throb and pulse, starts to empty in me, it feels like everything's being remade. Beautiful, perfect, brand new.

He collapses over me, stroking my hair, and I see his arm, right next to my face. Daddy Dom, the tattoo says.

And he is. But he's more than that. So much more.

CHAPTER TWENTY

DANE

I could stay like this forever. My girl next to me on my bed. My body tired but buzzing from the best sex of my life. Feels like for once, the whole world is in order.

We finally did it. Last night was incredible. The whole time I was with Harper, I kept worrying that I'd get some kind of dumb phone call, or someone would bang on the door, or something would explode. But, by some miracle, none of those things happened. Instead, there was a different kind of explosion. And this morning I feel like a changed man.

I gently slip out of bed, careful not to disturb Harper. I want her to get plenty of sleep — we were up *very* late last night.

I pad into the bathroom. I'm naked except for the cling film around my arm. I look at myself in the mirror, and unroll the clingfilm.

Daddy Dom.

I'm so fucking proud of this tattoo. And I'm proud of Harper for choosing it for me. Such a bold, exciting decision. She really knows me, really gets me.

The skin under the clingfilm is moist — perfect for healing a tattoo. Aftercare of a tattoo is the single most important way to ensure that the blacks stay black and the colors stay bright. I want this tattoo to last forever, black as the night, solid as my love for Harper.

That's what it is. Love.

I'm head over heels for her. When I said I needed her last night, I meant it.

I lean into the sink, put my arm under the hot tap, then, preparing myself, I turn it on. The water stings a bit, but it's not too bad. It's more the thought of it — the idea that I've got an open wound on my arm that I'm washing.

After I'm done, I get a clean towel and pat the raw skin dry, then I squeeze some diaper rash cream out onto my skin and rub it in, before wrapping my arm with more clingfilm.

'I love watching you do stuff.'

Harper's watching from the door.

'You're like a damn ninja,' I say. 'Silent and deadly.'

'Daddy you're naked,' she says.

'Damn,' I reply. 'You're right.' I reach up and scratch my head. 'I wonder how that happened. Whatever we did last night must have knocked out my few remaining brain cells.'

She rushes up to me, all smiles and giggles, and she wraps her arms around my waist.

'You've got lots of brain cells,' she says. 'At least three. Maybe even four on a good day.'

'Sounds about right,' I grin.

Her hand falls down my back, lands on my ass.

'You're so strong, Daddy. Never felt a body like yours before.'

'You keep touching me like that, you're gonna feel something else in a second,' I say. I can already feel my cock hardening as she keeps caressing my butt. She feels it too, looking down at it as it prods into her.

'Oh no,' she says, looking innocent. 'Wouldn't want that to happen.'

'So how come you're still stroking?' I ask, as my cock hardens so much that it's starting to get painful.

'I dunno,' she says. She pulls her hands round to the front, pulls

CHAPTER TWENTY

them over my abs, my chest, then, she lets them play with my coarse, dark pubic hair, twirling it round her fingers. She grazes my cock with her hand. 'Oops,' she says. 'I touched it.'

'Oops, huh?'

'Daddy,' she says, 'can you do something for me?'

'What?'

'I woke up thinking about it. It's gonna sound dumb. I just can't stop thinking about it.'

I laugh. 'What terrible thing are you gonna ask me to do.'

'Nothing bad,' she says. 'I just want you to slap my little face with your cock.'

Before I say anything, she kneels down, looks up at me with those angelic blue eyes. 'Please Daddy. I'll be sooo nice to you in return.'

I grab my cock, rub the tip against her cheek. 'That's what you want, is it?'

She nods. 'Just want to feel that heavy dick against my cheek.'

'Like this?' I say. I twist my hips and flick my thick cock against her face — not too hard, but it makes a satisfying slap sound.

'Thank you, Daddy,' she says, grinning wide.

I flick my cock again, sending the tip to Harper's face, but this time, before it hits, she turns her head round, and catches the tip of my manhood in her pretty little mouth.

'Naughty girl,' I say, as she starts to suck. She looks up at me, bats her eyelids, and takes me even further into her mouth. 'Fucking hell,' I say. Harper smiles, sucks more, lifts her hand up and cups my balls. The sensation is crazy. Her tongue flicks over my cock as my balls throb in her hand. She gently rolls them and then, she strokes the space behind my ball sack, massaging my perineum, making my cock pulse and throb.

'Where'd ya learn to do that?' I pant, as she takes my dick from her mouth. She kisses the tip, licks my shaft, then pops my balls into her mouth. She keeps moving her hand over my cock, pumping gently as her lips flit over my skin, making me hard as a rock, and fit to burst.

'I'll never tell,' she says, flicking that devilish tongue over the end of my cock.

'Put it back in,' I grunt, eager for relief.

She nods, and takes me in again. This time, I reach down, grab her hair, scrunch my fingers into it, and as she starts to bob back and forth, I move her head in time. She groans as I do so, and the vibration and sound is fucking ridiculous.

'God damn!' I say. 'How does this feel so fucking good?'

Harper grabs my body and pulls me close, taking me the deepest yet, and then, as I feel her lips start to grip, I feel my climax building. My head drops, my body shakes, and I come so damn hard I feel spots.

Harper looks up at me, a dreamy smile on her face. She moves off my cock, and with the dirtiest look I've ever seen, she swallows me all down.

'You taste good, Daddy.'

'What did I do to deserve you?' I ask.

'You saved me,' she says, simply. 'Not my life. My soul.'

*

'Two hours. That's it.'

'Two and a half?' Harper's wearing a sheep onesie, sitting on my couch. I've never negotiated TV watching time before. Maybe two hours is way too much time. That's like, enough time for a hundred cartoons, right?

'Two hours tops, Harper. Then we're looking at that business plan

CHAPTER TWENTY

again before the raid.'

I want to make today as much for Harper as possible. I know she's anxious about me going out tonight, so I wanna build up the good vibes.

'Okey-dokey,' she says. 'Baaa!' she adds.

That sheep onesie is the best investment I ever made. As soon as Harper put it on, it's like she turned *into* a cute little lamb.

'Right, what you gonna watch?' I ask.

'Do you have Spongebob?'

'I think so.' I reach for the remote, but as I do, I notice a message on my phone. Oh no. It's Margot. Fuck. I forgot.

'Uh, Harper,' I say. 'I've got something to do. Damn. I'm sorry honey, but I have to go out.'

She looks up at me, her lower lip quivering. 'You have to leave me?'

Fuck. I don't wanna leave Harper. But I can't abandon Margot. Shit. No-one knows about Margot. No-one in my life. Not Bud, not Hawk, no-one from Daddies MC.

I'm gonna have to tell her.

'Harper, maybe you can come with me.'

The look of disappointment on her face is crushing. But I can't back down.

'Don't wanna,' she says, crossing her arms. 'You promised.'

She's being bratty, but she's right. I did promise her.

'Please,' I say, 'come with me. You'll understand. You trust me, right?'

She nods. 'I do.'

I hold out my hand. 'I'm gonna show you my biggest secret. No-one else knows this. She's now the second most important thing in my life.'

'She?'

LUCKY MOON

*

My arms are laden with buckets of fried chicken. I kick open the wire door on the edge of Margot's complex.

'I wish you'd just tell me why we're here with all this food.' Harper's got two sharing bottles of coke.

I pause, put the buckets down on the ground for a second. We've been in such a rush, I've had no time to explain what's going on. I guess it's time to come clean.

'OK, look, you're about to meet someone amazing.'

'Margot?'

'Yes,' I say. 'Be nice to her. She's very special to me.'

'Another ex?' Harper says with a petulant look.

I shake my head. 'You honestly think I'd bring you to meet an ex? Come on, Harper, you know me better than that.'

She pokes out her lower lip.

'I told you that when I was a kid, I was in and out of foster homes quicker than a possum up a drainpipe. Most of my foster parents were assholes. Some beat me. Most shouted at me. Margot was the only one to ever treat me good.'

Her scowl softens.

'She even called me when I was in prison. I've been very careful since getting out not to involve her in my life. The reason that no-one from the club knows is that I don't want her to be a target. If she got hurt because of my lifestyle I'd never forgive myself.'

'That's so sweet,' Harper says, smiling softly.

'I decided that I was gonna do what I could to make her life a bit better. So once a week, I bring her food, and I eat with her. Haven't

CHAPTER TWENTY

missed a date in ten years. It's why I was so late for the drugs vote at the club.'

'You're a kind man,' Harper says.

I snort. 'Don't tell anyone. Right, come on. I'm nervous. Feels kinda like you're about to meet my mom.'

'I can't wait to meet her.'

We walk to the front door together. Margot lives in a tiny condo in the center of LA. She's been here for decades, and the neighborhood grew up while her tiny house stayed the same. I ring the doorbell, and seconds later, the door swings open.

'Dane, sweetie, I thought you'd forgotten me!' Her eyes twinkle, her short, white hair shines, her lips stretch wide in a smile.

'Never, Mags!' I say, giving her a big hug.

'Who's this little darling,' she says, looking over at Harper.

'Well,' I say. 'She's my Old Lady.'

'Old Lady?' say both Margot and Harper at the same time. I can see these two are gonna get on.

'That's what us bikers call our girlfriends.'

'You and your noisy bikes,' Margot says. 'When you gonna settle down and get a nice Lexus?'

'Never, Mags, never.'

'I'm pleased to meet you, Margot,' says Harper.

'You are cute as a button!' Margot cries. 'Come in, you two. I'm so hungry I'm gonna start chewing the furniture. Let's eat, let's talk, let's laugh!'

CHAPTER TWENTY-ONE

HARPER

'She is *amazing*!'

Lunch with Margot was incredible. Meeting someone who's known Dane for so long without being a member of Daddies MC was wonderful.

Don't get me wrong, I love all the guys at the club, but Margot couldn't be more different. She kept telling me stories about times that Dane had helped mow her lawn, and helped replace her AC, or the time he'd scared away the naughty man who tried to break into her garage.

'She's pretty special,' admits Dane. 'I owe her a lot. Sometimes I think it's because of her that I have any faith in humanity at all.'

'I can see why you keep her a secret, too. The thought of her getting hurt is just... awful. Don't worry, Daddy, I'll keep your secret.'

'I know you will. Now, we better get that onesie back on, because you've got some Spongebun to watch.'

I try to stifle a laugh.

'It's not Spongebun, is it?' he asks.

'It's Spongebob, Daddy. Spongebob Squarepants.'

'How could I ever forget?'

I don't have much time with Dane. Any second know, he's gonna go meet with his club brothers, and raid the Blood Fuckers.

We relax together on the couch. Dane puts his arm around me. 'Hey, speaking of buns, have you heard anything from superstar baker Frank recently?'

'Nope,' I say.

'Hmmm,' Dane says.

'That's a long hmm,' I reply.

Dane grabs the remote, and switches on the TV. 'Just thinking. I wonder what his involvement with the whole drug situation is. I hope he's alright.'

I feel ice drip down my spine. 'Why wouldn't he be?'

'Someone lost $50,000 worth of blow.'

'It wasn't his fault though.'

'Yeah. But the Blood Fuckers aren't gonna know that he's not the reason that their drugs are chilling out under my bed. If I were them, I'd have a pretty serious chat with him.'

Fuck. Frank's a douchebag, but I wouldn't want him to get hurt.

The intro music to my favorite cartoon starts up, but I can't get into it. I keep thinking about Frank, in trouble, not having anyone to help.

'I hope he's OK,' I say.

'Me too,' says Dane. Since we got back, he's been tense. I can tell he's focused on the raid. I wonder what it's like in his head. Whether he's running scenarios through in his head, or whether he's just kind of meditating, getting ready for whatever's gonna happen. 'By the way, I organized something for you while you're out.'

'Oh?'

'I saw how well you got on with Babs, so I thought you might want a play date. She's coming around. With Titus, one of the other guys from the club. They'll be looking after you.'

'Eeeee!'

'You excited to see me go, huh?'

'No!' I say. 'It's just, I *did* like Babs. She's so cool. Way too cool for me. Do I know Titus?'

'Nope,' he says. 'But I do. He's a good man, and I know he'll look after the two of you in case anything goes down. Not that I'm expecting

CHAPTER TWENTY-ONE

it to.'

'Sounds good,' she says.

'Good.'

There's a sudden, urgent bang on the door.

'What the f-'

Dane leaps up, eyes fixed on the door.

'Open up, Dane, it's me.' I recognize the voice, but can't put it to a face.

'Bud?' Dane says, as he heads over. He opens the door. Bud's there. He doesn't look drunk today. He looks sober and serious.

'Glad you're here. We have to go. Now.'

'Now? Where?'

'Blood Fuckers HQ.' Bud rubs his nose, snorts.

'Bud, how d'you know about today? I thought you weren't getting involved.'

'Course I'm involved, son. It's my fucking club. I'm involved in everything that goes down. Been thinking a lot about you. Think you're right. We can't afford to have these assholes bringing drugs into our neighborhood. Innocent people are getting hurt. That's not what we're about.'

Dane smiles so broad that for a second, it looks like he's a little kid.

'That's good news,' he says. 'Nah, that's great news!' He claps Bud on the shoulder.

'I'm gonna help. I found out that there's a deal going down at the HQ. Now. Like in half an hour. I've spoken to Hawk, and Ripper. Well done for talking to Rock. Glad you two put that squabble behind you.'

'Shit, Bud, looks like you're firing on all cylinders.'

'Damn straight.'

'Just a minute. I'm gonna make sure Harper's OK, then we'll hit the road.'

He scoots back across to me, crouches down and looks me in the eye. 'OK babe, this is it. I'll be back soon, I hope. Remember, Babs and Titus should be here soon. Til then, you're allowed to watch as much Bunbob as you like.'

I laugh.

'Got you,' he says, kissing my forehead. 'I know it's Spongebun.'

'You're so silly, Daddy,' I say, wrapping my arms around him. He kisses me slow and deep, pulls me up off the couch, cradling me in his arms.

'You stay cute for me, Darling.'

'You stay perfect for me,' I reply.

He puts me down, blows me a kiss, and steps out of the apartment. And as he leaves, I get the strangest feeling. Like I'm never gonna see him again.

*

There's only so many episodes of Spongebob you can watch before you go completely crazy. Even I, as a Little, find it tough going after the fourth.

I've got Pudding here with me, and he's snuggled up on the couch next to me.

'Who does live in a pineapple under the sea?' I ask pudding.

I keep checking my phone, hoping to hear something from Dane, or, at least, from Babs and Titus. But so far, nothing at all.

I wonder how the raid's going. I wonder whether it's started.

Suddenly, I hear something. A voice — and not coming from the TV. I mute the show, watch as Spongebob yammers something at Gary,

CHAPTER TWENTY-ONE

listen as carefully as I can. Moments later, I hear the voice again. It's actually voices — a man and a woman. He's talking low and she's giggling.

It's gotta be Titus and Babs. Sure enough, a couple second later, there's an urgent rap at the door.

I jump up, look at myself in the mirror, stick my tongue out, then head for the door.

But when I open it, it's not Titus and Babs. When I see who it is, all the wind rushes from my lungs, like I've been punched in the gut.

Because standing outside my Daddy's apartment, grinning like lunatics, are Baby and Darlin'. I open to mouth to scream, but like in a nightmare, no sound comes out.

'How you doin', cutie?' Baby says. 'Thought we'd come pay you a visit.'

'Aren't you gonna invite us in?' Darlin' says, before stepping confidently over the threshold. I glance over at the couch, over at my phone. There's no way I can get there in time, no way I can call 911. Fuck fuck fuck, what do I do?

'Where are Titus and Babs?' I say, my voice hoarse and quiet.

'Change of plan, bitch,' Baby spits. 'We're your new babysitters. Don't worry, we're gonna take real good care of you.' He licks his lips, leaving a slimy trail of spittle around his stubbly mouth.

'What are you gonna do?' I feel my heart drop to my stomach, fear totally engulfing me.

'We're gonna play hide and go seek,' says Darlin'. I *hate* her. First, she's gorgeous, in that filthy, dirty way that only really *cool* girls can be. Second, she's confident — so confident it makes me sick.

Even though she's clearly a horrible person, I kinda want to be her. I know, I know, I hate myself. I just can't help it. She takes a pouch of tobacco from a pocket, and starts stuffing it into… something?

Is that a pipe?

She lights the pipe, and gouts of thick black smoke start to fill Dane's place. It's so disrespectful, and I feel a quick pang of shame, as though I should be doing something. But what am I meant to do? There's two of them, and only one of me. And it's not like I'm a fighter.

I'm just a scared little girl, cowering in a toilet cubicle, never wanting to come out.

'You're gonna tell us where you hid our drugs,' Darlin' says, blowing more smoke out. 'And you're gonna tell us right now.'

Oh shit. They know. Somehow, they know.

Frank must have told them. Poor Frank.

'I don't know what you mean.'

There's a hollow click. I turn and look at Baby. He's holding a gun straight at my head.

My breathing spikes. I feel the heave of my chest I try, desperately, to regain control of my body. Suddenly, I hear Dane in my head.

Just tell them, Harper. Don't be stupid. I'll never forgive you if you get yourself hurt. Don't be a hero. Stay alive.

I'm sure it's what he'd want me to do. Positive. But for some reason, I just can't bring myself to do it.

'Don't hurt me,' I say, cowering away from the gun. 'Please, let me go. I don't know anything about any drugs.'

Before I can react, Baby steps forward, and cracks the gun across my jaw. The pain is unlike anything I've ever felt before — so sharp it almost feels cold. Then, a moment later, it really hits — an insane torrent of agony. My face throbs and I feel tears on my cheek.

'No games, cunt. Next time, it's not gonna be the butt of the gun. Next time, I fucking kill you.'

CHAPTER TWENTY-ONE

'Baby, I love it when you use the 'c' word,' Darlin' says, blowing a smoke ring across the room.

Baby grins. 'I'mma plow you so damn hard later tonight, Darlin',' he says. Darlin' slinks across the room, throwing those hips from side to side with each step.

'I know it,' she says, then she pushes those smoky lips against his. Baby doesn't close his eyes. He keeps them trained on me.

'Now,' he says, when they finish their kiss. 'I think you were deciding whether or not you felt like dying today.'

'I'll tell you,' I say. 'They're under the bed.'

'Darlin' go check,' Baby barks.

She does as he asks, heading into the bedroom. Less than a minute later, she's back, holding the bricks of cocaine in her hands, grinning her head off.

'You dumb bitch,' Baby says. 'I was never gonna kill you. You know that, right?'

I half expected it. But to hear him taunt me like is so cruel. My cheeks burn, my eyes sting.

'Just let me go,' I sob. 'You've got what you wanted.'

Darlin' shakes her head. She takes another puff of the pipe, then tips the ash out onto the floor. 'You're what we wanted,' she says. She reaches into her pocket again, pulls out a length of black satin. 'There's no way that we're going to let our bait go. That would make no sense at all.'

Bait? What does she mean?

'Come on, Harper. It's time for your photoshoot.'

CHAPTER TWENTY-TWO

DANE

It feels so good to have Bud riding at my side again. It's been too long. He revs his hog as we stream down South Central Avenue, fast and proud.

I'm following ten feet behind. I've been worried about Bud for a while now. The past year or so, he's been more distant, less engaged, less interested in club happenings — which isn't like him at all. But recently, the last few months he's been really bad — drinking heavily, even got into a couple brawls at The Milk Shed.

Tonight though, seeing him focused and clear-headed, it kinda feels like the old Bud is back.

He signals up ahead, and a moment later, pulls his hog over to the sidewalk. I draw up alongside him, turn my engine off. The street's empty save for streetlamps and colored light spilling out of convenience stores and late-night bars.

'The place is a couple blocks from here,' he says. 'Thought we'd walk the last couple minutes, draw a little less attention to ourselves.'

'Good thinking,' I say.

'You come packing anything?'

I nod. 'Got ol' reliable in a back holster.'

'Good,' he says. 'What's your plan?'

'Me, Rock, and Hawk were gonna sneak in. Rock's bringing rope. We're gonna knock the guards out, one by one. Then, we take whatever's going on in the warehouse. Can't be that many of them.'

He nods.

'Way these things normally go down,' he says, 'shouldn't be more than two on each side. Four baddies in total.'

'Right,' I say. 'Once we've got everything, all the evidence we need, Rock's got a contact — a trustworthy contact — on the LAPD. We'll call it in, and leave them all trussed up.'

'Good,' he says. 'I like it. Low-violence is good. Cause whatever's left of the Blood Fucker's will be mad after this. Could be all-out war.'

'Specially if we bag Satan,' I say.

Bud raises his eyebrows. 'Really think you'll have a chance at that?'

'I'm betting we will.'

'What makes you say that?' he says. He glances left and right as we walk, checking for any sides of trouble.

'He's a control freak,' I say.

Bud snorts. 'No-one knows who the fuck he is,' he says.

'Exactly. He's managed that carefully over the years. That means he's involved in *everything*. In every part of the Blood Fuckers organization. There's no way that someone that obsessed with secrecy and success is gonna miss a deal like this.'

Bud nods. 'Reckon you could be right. You're a smart kid,' he says. 'I'm proud of you. Always figured you'd take over from me as president one day.'

'Damn,' I say. 'Always thought Ripper would be a better fit.'

'I like Ripper, but... you're my boy.'

It's the first time he's ever said anything like this to me. In the past, he's always been so reserved. So harsh. There's something different about him today. 'Thanks Bud. That means a lot.'

After a couple more minutes, we arrive at the address. It's an apartment a couple story's up in s dingy back alley. To my surprise, there are three Blood Fuckers, just waiting on the street by the entrance.

'You sure you wanna do this?' he says. His voice sounds different.

CHAPTER TWENTY-TWO

More urgent.

'Whaddya mean?' I reply.

'They've got numbers. Maybe we should just forgot about this.'

'We can't forget about it, Bud. This is our chance to take 'em down.'

'Hear me out. If we hit the Blood Fuckers Today, they'll just hit us tomorrow. Especially if we take out Satan. What's stopping us from going back to the Milk Shed. We can pick up the cocaine from your place and sell it — just this once.'

My eyes narrow. I can barely believe what he's saying.

'Then,' he replies, 'we give the money to charity. To the poor, to the needy — fuck knows there's enough of them in the Fashion District. We keep ten percent, cover our costs, and we carry on. Protecting the innocent, but staying safe, too.'

'Bud, you know what I'm gonna say, don't you?'

He looks at me. Sighs. 'I know. You're too good. Too pure. Fine. We'll do it. I told Hawk and Rock to wait round the back. You might wanna go join them.'

'What are you gonna do?' I ask, confused.

'I'm heading back to the Milk Shed, gonna rustle up some reinforcements. This is obviously an even bigger deal than we thought — otherwise they wouldn't have all that muscle up front. You guys go in, and I'll be here with some heavies in ten minutes.'

I nod. 'OK, that sounds sensible.'

'Good,' he says. 'Just be careful until I'm back. But if I know you the way I think I do, I doubt you're gonna take my advice.'

I nod. 'See you soon, Bud. Hurry, or there won't be anything for you guys to do.'

He gives me a salute, then heads back to his bike.

I get out my phone, look at a map of the area, then I walk to my left, heading round the back of the apartment block.

I can't get this niggling feeling out of my gut, like something's wrong here tonight. I can't quite put my finger on it. Then, I get this horrible feeling, and I have to text Harper. I pull out my phone and text her, 'You OK Baby? Things about to kick off here. Wanted to check in on you. If I'm not back, make sure you do your affirmations before bed.'

I asked Babs and Titus to stay over. Hope that Harper won't feel too self-conscious to do her affirmations with them around. They won't judge her, but I get that it might be more difficult for her with other people around.

As I walk, I keep checking my phone. Nothing comes through. Just as I'm starting to get worried, a reply flashes up on the screen.

'I'm good, Daddy. I won't forget. Can't wait to see you! I'm having an amazing time — Babs is so much fun!'

Huh. It's a perfect normal message. Nice, even. It's just… a little bit off. Should I be worried? Should I forget this and head straight back to my place? No. It's fine. There's nothing weird about the message.

Ugh. My head's all over the place.

'Dane!' It's Rock's voice, a strained whisper from up ahead. I have to do this. I'm sure Harper is fine. It's just the stress of running this operation getting to me.

I raise my finger to my lips, and catch sight of them. I glance up — the building's back is pretty standard. There's a fire escape snaking its way round towards the third story. That's our way in.

'Gentlemen,' I say. 'Good to see you.'

Hawk claps his hand into mine, and Rock gives me a respectful nod.

'Where's Bud?' Hawk asks, shooting me a concerned glance.

CHAPTER TWENTY-TWO

'Gone to get back up. We should probably get going though. Deal's due to go down any minute. We don't want to miss anything.'

'How's the ink healing up?' Rock asks.

'You got new ink?' Hawk asks, a grin on his face.

'Show him, Dane.'

I roll up my sleeve, revealing the cling-film over the ink. The artwork is clearly visible.

'Fuck!' Hawk says, clearly impressed. 'That is *badass* Dane. So you've accepted who you are?'

I nod. 'I always had this idea about what a Daddy Dom is. Someone who is a big BDSM guy, into whipping and talking shit to his Little. I never really got it until I met Harper. Never felt protective until I met her. Never felt like myself until I met her.'

'You've really fallen for her, haven't you?' Hawk asks.

'Mmmhmm.'

'You old softy,' Rock laughs. 'You'll never see me settle down with just one girl.'

'You know what,' I say. 'You might think that now, but I tell you, when you meet the right woman, no-one else will ever be good enough.'

'Whatever,' Rock says.

'Bet you a hundred bucks,' I say.

'How would I ever win that bet?' he replies.

'Simple. If you're single at the end of next year, I'll give you a hundred bucks. It'll be a good Christmas for you.' I don't know why I'm making this insane bet. Something's changed in me, and it's all down to Harper.

'Taken,' Rock says. 'Now, let's get fucking going.' He pulls out a comb, pulls it back through his hair.

'Fucking poser!' says Hawk.

Rock winks. 'Gotta look good before you stop a drug deal, Dane.'

'Speaking of which... how do we get up onto the fire escape?'

'You know how you were saying you're not into whipping subs?' Rock asks. Before I have time to answer, he pulls out a long, coiled bull-whip from behind his back.

'Are you fucking kidding me?' I ask.

Hawk is too busy chuckling to say anything — damn knucklehead.

'I hope you're ready to see something pretty fucking special,' Rock grunts. 'Been practicing. Spent a lot of time in the Nursery with some very willing, very naughty girls who helped me with my wrist technique.'

'Just get on with it, Indiana Jones.'

I don't quite know what he's planning to do. Is he gonna wrap the whip around something and pull himself up? I doubt even he's strong enough to do something like that.

He eyes up the fire-escape, and pulls the whip back behind him.

'This is ridiculous,' Hawk says. But then, Rock does something insane. He flicks the whip through quickly, sending the tip all the way up to the fire escape. It whips around something I hadn't even seen — the release lever for a ladder.

A moment later, with a tug of his wrist, the lever clunks open, sending the ladder plummeting down to street level. The ladder screeches as it falls, and I'm instantly on high alert. We all duck back into the alley, and I'm fully expecting a bunch of bikers to stream out the apartment block.

But the bikers don't come.

'What the fuck?' I ask.

'I guess they didn't hear?' Rock says.

We wait a minute, and then, approach the ladder.

CHAPTER TWENTY-TWO

'You got the lock pick?'

Hawk grins. 'Always.'

Before he settled down in the garage, Hawk used to boost cars and bikes, all around LA. He claims that there's not a lock that he can't open. I hope he's not been overstating his skill.

'Remember, check the damn window first. Make sure we go into an empty room, OK?'

Hawk nods. He goes up first, with me second, and Rock bringing up the rear. By the time I arrive up at the window to the apartment on the third floor, Hawk's already started picking.

'This won't take long,' he whispers.

There's no light on at all inside the apartment — not even coming through from another room. That's weird. Hawk looks at me. 'You ready to go in?'

I nod, then I draw my gun from behind my back. I don't want to have to use this thing, but I want to be ready, just in case. Rock's already got his piece out.

The window slides quietly up, and Hawk steps into the place. It's quiet. Totally quiet.

'Something's wrong,' I say, in my normal voice. I already know — this place is empty. It's a fucking setup.

My fears are confirmed when I push open the door. It's an empty, unfurnished apartment.

'What's going on?' Rock asks, definite concern in his voice.

My phone vibrates. When I look at the screen, I feel sick.

It's a photo of Harper. A gag in her mouth. Tears streaming down her cheeks.

There's a message with the photo, as well as a link to a location on google maps.

'Come meet us. Be here within half an hour, or Harper dies. Daddy.'

Something roils in my heart. Not fear. Not anxiety.

Pure, unbridled rage. Whoever is responsible for this just made the biggest mistake of their life. No-one fucks with my Little and lives.

CHAPTER TWENTY-THREE

HARPER

I don't know where I am. The blindfold is pulled tight across my eyes, and my hands are bound tight behind me.

I think I'm in the back of a van. I can hear the rumble of the engine, feel the bump of the tires on the road underneath me. Where are they taking me?

I tug at my bonds, hoping desperately that I'll be able to somehow wrench my arms free. Obviously, there's no way. Baby tied me so tight, it feels like the circulation to my hands has been cut off.

I'm terrified. Not just about what's gonna happen to me. Because I know that the real target of all this is Dane. I don't know what they've got planned, but I know it's not gonna be good.

There's the sound of voices every now and then — Baby's ugly growl and Darlin's equally unsettling laugh. Occasionally, I catch the acrid smell of pipe smoke. I imagine Darlin's bright red lips around that thing, imagine the smoke filling the cab of the van.

Never in my whole life did I ever think that I'd be kidnapped like this. All I've ever wanted to do is be a baker, make tasty cakes. I feel like I should be coming up with a plan — some kind of insane escape attempt. But no matter what scenarios I keep running through what I could do: some kind of backflip that ends up with me blindly kicking Darlin's head off. The truth is though, that I've got no chance. I'm just going to do the only thing I can: sit in the back of this van until I get carried out.

The shame I'm feeling right now is intense. Not only did I not put up a fight when they came to abduct me, but when Dane had sent a message through, I helped them write a reply. I mean sure, they held a gun to my head and forced me to do it, but if Dane gets hurt, I don't know what I'll do.

Eventually, after around ten minutes, the van comes to a halt. I hear the clunk and whine of the door opening and I feel the fresh air on my arms.

This is it.

'Get up, bitch.' It's Baby's voice — cold and nasty. I drag myself up from the floor, stumble to my feet. 'Come on, get out. We've got places to go. People to see.'

Darlin' chuckles in the background.

'Aren't you gonna help me out?' I ask.

'You don't need help,' replies Baby. 'You just need to hurry the fuck up.'

I step forward, trying to feel to my way to the doorway, but before I manage, I feel a tug forward. I tumble down, feel the smack of the asphalt into my face. My jaw stings again, and I feel pain in my leg, too.

'Enjoy your trip?' Darlin' asks, from somewhere nearby.

Don't cry, don't cry, don't cry, I think to myself. I wish I had Pudding here with me. I need something for comfort — anything. My heart hurts more than my body.

A strong, vice-like hand grips my arm, wrenching my up. 'I told you to hurry, didn't I? Don't have time for you to fuck around.' He drags me forward, and I try to keep up, following his footsteps, until finally, he pulls me up a staircase.

I try to focus on my surroundings, desperate to try to take in anything — any tiny detail that could help me in future. But there's nothing. The only thing that's a vague clue is the smell — the acrid scent of chemicals, something like bleach, but far, far worse.

CHAPTER TWENTY-THREE

But by the time I'm bundled into a warm room somewhere up a single story, I still have no idea where I am.

'You stay here,' Baby says. 'We've got someone special for you to meet. Someone who's excited to see you. Don't do anything stupid, now.'

I hear the two of them as they leave the room, and that's when the situation really hits me. I'm alone in here, and no-one's coming to save me.

But I'm not alone for long. Just a couple minutes later, I hear shuffling feet and then what sounds like a body hitting the floor.

'Thought you two might want to catch up,' Darlin' says, laughing. Then, I hear the sound of a door locking shut.

'Harper? Is that you?'

Oh my god.

'Frank?'

I feel fingers on my face, and then, finally, the blindfold is off my face. I'm in a tiny room — kinda like a broom cupboard. There's nothing in here, except for Frank.

At first sight, I don't even recognize him. Half his face is one big, angry bruise. His eye is so puffy he can barely open it, and, when he smiles at me, I see that he's missing a couple teeth.

'Harper, I'm so happy to see you.'

'Frank,' I reply, 'what happened? What did they do to you?'

'What do you think?' he grimaces.

'You poor thing.'

'Me? What about you? They hurt you? Hit your face?'

I nod.

'Those bastards. They promised me that nothing bad would happen to me. They promised that they wouldn't harm a single hair on your head.'

'How did this happen, Frank?' I ask. 'How did you get caught up in this?'

I've never seen him like this before. Never seen this emotion before, this depth of feeling.

'Oh Harper,' he says. 'If you could know what I've been through. The things I've had to keep from you. I'm so sorry. I've treated you like a piece of trash. I've acted like a damn monster.'

'It's OK,' I say, 'I didn't know what was going on.'

He looks me in the eye. 'Superstar Frosting has been in money trouble for some time. It's not cheap to keep a business running in LA, especially with the economy being what it is. Couple years ago, we nearly went under.'

'I had no idea.'

'No one did,' he laughs. 'Except the Blood Fuckers. They loaned me money. A lot of money. Only catch was that I had to do a favor every now and then.'

'A favor?'

'Yep. To start, the favors weren't so bad. Had to keep a pallet of 'something' in the bakery for a couple days. Had to turn a blind eye to some dealing that went on outside the bakery. Then the demands got a bit more extreme. Time came for me to pay back the debt, see. So they got serious.'

'They got you smuggling drugs, didn't they?'

He nodded.

'They figured that no-one would suspect the most famous baking company in Los Angeles of being involved with the drug trade. And I guess they were right. Thing is, though, I paid back my debt. Months ago. But the demands just ramped up. Got worse.'

CHAPTER TWENTY-THREE

He looks so damn sad. So defeated.

'I don't run a bakery any more. I'm a gangster. You're not the only one moving this stuff around. I've had to hire a fleet of damn drivers. But you're the one that hurts me the most. Because you're such a talented damn baker.'

'Really?' It's a moment of light in this dark situation.

'Course. Why d'ya think I didn't want you baking at the shop? I didn't want all the others to see how good you were. Partly because I didn't want to have to pay you a proper wage. Couldn't afford to.'

It's all starting to make sense now. The sudden change in his personality. The mood swings. The crazy, bursts of anger and pain.

'The whole time I worked for you, I would have given anything to hear you say these things to me.'

'I know,' he says. 'Of course I know. Maybe if you'd met me ten years ago, if I'd been your boss then, I coulda been good to you. Helped you to develop. Sorry I failed you so badly.'

It feels like now, at his lowest point, he's speaking the most freely I've ever heard him speak.

'You've been through a lot,' I say, trying to soothe him. But it's no use.'

He slumps down in the corner. 'Doesn't excuse what I did. Exploited you. Turned you into a slave. I shoulda fired you. That was the only way I could have kept you safe. If it hadn't been for that guy — Dane — I probably woulda.'

'Dane?' My heart pounds. 'What did Dane do?'

'The day after you were meant to deliver that cake to the Chinese Theater. He called me. Threatened me. Told me that if I fired you, there would be trouble. Assumed he was from the Blood Fuckers. If it hadn't been for him, I'd have got rid of you.'

Is it possible that Dane — my Daddy — is somehow involved with this? It can't be. He must have been trying to save my job. To protect me. But there's something, in the back of my mind, a niggling, writhing doubt — the first one I've really had about Dane.

And I can't shake it.

'I'm gonna find a way,' he says. 'Find a way to make up for the nightmare I put you through. Somehow, I'm gonna make this right.'

He's shaking his head, lost in his own world.

'They're gonna kill me,' he continues. 'For losing those drugs. They're gonna kill me.' He looks up. 'And you too. I'm sorry. They don't need us any more. No point.'

'Why would they kill us?' I say.

'Why wouldn't they?'

The words hang in the air, hollow, but amazingly heavy. For a moment, we sit there in silence, thinking about the situation, thinking about the awfulness of everything.

Suddenly, a knock on the door breaks us out of our silence.

'Can I come in?'

I recognize the voice, but I don't know who it belongs to. The way I feel right now — like none of this is real, like none of this is happening — the voice might well be from a dream.

Frank looks up. 'I'm sorry babe. I'm so sorry.'

Even that, the way he says it, is kinda dream-like. Maybe, any second, I'm gonna wake up. And my Daddy will be there, lying next to me, his big arms around me. All my worries, all my doubts will just drift away. But when the door opens, and I see the face of the man behind it, I know that I'm not in a dream.

I'm stuck in a nightmare.

CHAPTER TWENTY-FOUR

DANE

This place is the real deal. Soon as we're nearby, I know that this has to be the heart of the Blood Fucker operation in LA.

The warehouse is in Pasadena, far to the North of the center of Los Angeles. As we approach on foot — we left our bikes ten minutes ago to ensure a silent approach — I see guards everywhere. These aren't like the guys outside the apartment complex, either.

All of them have guns, and they all look serious. One on each entrance, seemingly all the way around.

'Any more word back from Bud?' Rock asks, when he sees the BF presence at the warehouse.

'Nothing yet,' I say. 'I sent him the new location, and he said he'd be on the way. Feels like this is gonna be an all-out war.'

Much as I hate the thought of it — especially the thought that blood might be spilled tonight — I'm driven by the need to save Harper. To drag her out of this shitty situation I've put her in.

'Here's the plan,' I say. 'It's the way it's gonna go down, and I don't want any argument, OK? This is all my fault, and I'm not having you guys get put in trouble. This whole thing is down to me.'

'Fuck that, Dane. We all voted for this. We want to help.' Hawk's voice is strong, his passion is clear.

'I get that,' I say, 'and you're gonna help. Just not straight away. Trust me — in the end, this is the way it's gotta go down.'

'What's the plan, boss?' Rock says.

'I'm going in. The front. No fucking around. I'm gonna turn myself in.'

'What?'

'Hear me out. The three of us have no chance against the whole fucking gang. It's suicide.'

'How is you turning yourself over not suicide?' Hawk asks.

'I've got something they want. The drugs in my place. It's not the whole stash. I had two bricks of cocaine at the bar, just in case. Never told Harper. Bout thirty grand's worth. They won't kill me while that's out there.'

'They'll beat you senseless,' Hawk says. 'Even if they don't kill you on purpose, might end up dying by accident.'

'I'm willing to take that chance. You guys wait for Bud to show up with the cavalry. When they're here, you storm the place — that entrance there, onto the main floor. I'm willing to bet that this is where they're cutting all the coke.'

'No doubt,' Rock says. 'I guess we just gotta hope that Bud doesn't take too long.'

'He won't. I trust him. With my life.'

Hawk nods. Before I go, I lean in to the two of them, embrace them.

'The minute they arrive,' I say, 'you gotta move. I don't know how things are gonna go down in there.'

They nod. 'Good luck, Dane,' Hawk says.

'I don't need luck. I've got my brothers.'

I turn, and I walk into the lions' den.

*

'Where's the rest of you?' The grunt on the door isn't the sharpest tool in the book. Dunno what I was expecting from a BF, but still.

'Got no-one with me,' I reply. My hands are up over my head, my

CHAPTER TWENTY-FOUR

gun holstered behind me. 'Came, just like the message said. I'm here in exchange for Harper, simple as that.'

He holds up his walkie talkie, barks the information I've just given him into it. A moment later, a reply. Sounds like Baby.

'Frisk him, bring him in,' he says.

I'd been expecting this. He's gonna find my gun, that's a gimme. But there's a chance he won't find my knife.

He points the barrel of his gun at me, and comes in close. I feel his hands on my sides, on my pockets, then, a moment later, he finds the holster on my back.

'Take it off, get it down on the fucking ground,' he says. His voice is trembling. Maybe I could make a move, take him out, run in all guns blazing.

No. It would be dumb. Too much of a fucking risk. Everything in the world is at stake right now. I have to play this safe.

I reach round, undo the holster, slowly, gently, lower it down to the ground with my shotgun inside.

'Right,' he says, 'let's fucking go.'

Soon as we enter the warehouse, the stench of ammonia hits me. There's no doubt, this is where they cut the drugs. If we could destroy this warehouse, burn it down, the Blood Fucker drug operation in LA would be crippled, at least for months, maybe permanently.

Primary mission objective: save Harper.

Secondary mission objective: destroy this nest of evil.

We walk through a small entranceway, and then we're in the factory floor. I see a horrific scene — wretched, dirty people, at filthy desks, working — forced to work. Some of these people are young — barely adults. There are women, older people, and they all look in terrible health.

I heard that the Blood Fuckers were involved with people trafficking as well as drugs, and now it all makes sense. This is slavery, pure and simple.

As I walk past, the workers look up at me with desperate faces. Some have looks of sympathy. Do they think that I'm gonna be joining them soon? Do they know why I'm here?

'Eyes ahead, asswipe,' the Blood Fucker says, digging me in the ribs with the butt of his assault rifle. I barely even flinch — I'm too wrapped up in the horrific scene ahead of me. But it wouldn't help me to get injured now, so I do as he asks, and keep my eyes ahead.

We leave the factory floor and head to a staircase.

'Boss has asked to see you,' he says. 'Not many people get an audience with Satan.'

Damn, I didn't realize I was being taken straight to the man in charge. And I've still got my knife in my pocket. Maybe I could end this all tonight.

'I'm honored,' I reply.

'Must have really fucking irritated him,' the grunt says. 'He's normally very reclusive.'

'So I hear,' I say.

I'm logging this route in my mind, making sure that if I need to get out of here at speed, I won't make any wrong turns. But there's not much further to go, because a moment later, we're outside a door, and then, the grunt knocks.

'Someone here to see you, boss.'

'Come on in.'

Oh fuck. Oh no. I know that voice. It can't be. It can't fucking be.

The door swings open. I feel like I've been smacked in the guts by a hammer. Then, a second later, I feel something with such detail and

CHAPTER TWENTY-FOUR

specificity that it's insane: my heart breaks in my chest.

'Son. Good to see you.'

Bud's sitting behind the desk. He's wearing a leather vest I've never seen him wear before. There's a Blood Fuckers patch on his shoulder. Buds' holding a leather leash, and it's tied round Harper's throat. There's a lurid bruise on her chin. I feel sick — a rising tide of nausea that threatens to sweep me away.

'Bud?' I say. The word catches in my throat. I feel like I'm gonna fall over.

'Sit down, Son. We've got a lot to catch up on.'

I can't talk. I can't think. I can't breathe.

'Come on,' he continues, 'sit down.'

Harper's looking up at me with desperation in her eyes. She must think I'm going to save her. To make everything alright. Well maybe this time I can't.

That's when it hits me. Backup isn't coming. No-one's bringing the rest of the Daddies MC.

It's just me. Sure, Rock and Hawk are outside, but what can they do? This is fucked. All my plans, the drugs I stashed away as a bargaining chip — all of that is irrelevant now.

Come on, Dane, think.

'I'm not gonna sit down,' I say.

'Suit yourself,' Bud replies, raising an eyebrow. He's sober now. Of course he fucking is. How could I know him for so long, and not really know him?

'Take that off Harper,' I say. 'Take it off right now.'

'Or what?' he says. 'I think she looks nice like this. Best place for a Little is on the end of a strong man's leash. Ain't that right, sweetheart?' He tugs the leather lash, pulls her towards him by the throat.

'Why, Bud? What's the point of it all?'

'The point of what?'

'This double life. You were like a father to me. You were a good man.'

He shakes his head. 'You don't get it, do you? You always were dumb. Always so fucking naive. Where do you think the money for all the shit that Daddies MC does comes from? You really think that a garage and a nightclub pays for it all? Where do you think the money for your bar came from?'

'You mean you've been running the Blood Fuckers for all this time? Siphoning money into Daddies MC?'

'Of course,' he says. 'All for you. And the other boys. I did the dirty work, so you all could stay pure. Play at being vigilantes. Clean your bikes. I kept the ugly side of the world from you, Dane. Tried to protect you. But you had to keep pushing.'

My brain's reeling. Then it hits me: Bud actually thinks he's a good guy.

'This is insane,' I say. 'You actually think that you've been good to me? Running Daddies MC like some kind of twisted charity? Some fucking gangster's hobby?'

'What's insane,' he roars, 'is you stealing my fucking drugs, stealing my money, and expecting there not to be any repercussions.'

'I thought you hated drugs,' I say. 'You know what they did to my paren—'

'I know better than you fucking know!' he roars. 'Don't talk to me about your parents. Don't talk to me about the sacrifices I made for you.' He lurches to his feet, draws a pistol from his belt, holds it, shaking, straight at my head.

His arm trembles, he sniffs. Snorts. Holy fuck. He's not sober. He's

CHAPTER TWENTY-FOUR

high.

I shake my head. 'So what now, Bud? You've got me here. Got the only woman I've ever loved at your feet.' I glance down at Harper — she's wracked with grief, her beautiful face twisted in anguish as I rage against Bud. 'What you gonna do now? You gonna shoot me?'

'I'm gonna give you a choice,' he says. 'Right now, my boys are outside, rounding up Hawk and Rock. No one's coming from the other club to save your asses. So you've got two options.' He lowers the gun. 'You can forget about the other club. Forget about living that fake fucking life. Forget being a boy scout, and join me. Be the son that you always could have been.' He lifts his arm again, points the gun straight at my heart. 'Or, you can die. Nothing's gonna threaten the organization I've built here, not even you.'

There's only one thing I can do. If Harper wasn't here, I'd defy Bud til the end. But I can't let her get hurt. It's the most painful decision of my life, and I know that in making this choice, Harper will never want to be with me again.

I open my mouth, and I'm about to speak, when there's a crazy sound from outside the door. It sounds like someone being strangled.

'What the fuck?' Bud grunts. Then, the door bursts in. It's Frank — but I barely recognize him. He's screaming and I see that his leg is bleeding. When Harper sees him, she lets out a muffled cry, and tries to go to him, but Frank doesn't look at her, he just jumps straight for Bud.

Bud snarls, points, pulls the trigger.

Frank hits the deck, inches from Bud. He didn't have time to get to him, didn't have time to take him down.

But he's bought me enough time. Just enough.

I'm low, I'm quick, I'm surging forward. The knife's in my hand, and before Bud can bring the gun to bare on me, I'm slashing, cutting his hand. He yelps, swears, cringes back, and I'm on top of him, pinning him down.

He's strong but I'm stronger. He's tough, but I'm tougher.

The knife's at his throat and I push it, hold it there.

'Wait!' he screams. 'You can't do this! There's something you have to know!'

'What?' I sneer. 'You're even more of an asshole than I already think?'

He grins a sick, twisted grin. 'Dane. I'm your fucking dad.'

CHAPTER TWENTY-FIVE

HARPER

Dane's staring at Bud like he's been slapped in the face. His knife is at the older man's throat, held so tight I keep squirming, worrying that he's gonna accidentally slip and kill him.

His father.

'You're fucking lying!' It sounds like a challenge, a statement, but I know that Dane's asking a question.

'You know I'm not,' he says. 'Fuck. I wish it was a lie. I wish I wasn't such a fuck-up. But it's true. When your mom died-'

'Don't talk about my mom!'

'When Yolande died, it hit me hard.' Something about hearing his mom's name calms Dane. He's breathing heavy, still on the edge of mania, but he's looking at Bud with softness in his eyes.

I glance over at Frank, fearing the worst. There's a pool of blood under him, but it looks like he's actually breathing. I wonder how long he's got before things go really bad for him.

'You were so young. I was so dumb. I was an addict, just like her. And I vowed to turn my life around. I vowed that instead of the drugs ruling me, I was gonna use them to rule the world. But that life didn't have space for a kid.'

I can feel Bud trying to manipulate Dane. I don't know if he's telling the truth about being Dane's dad — I don't even know if it matters — but I can tell a snake when I see one. I knew it in the bar when I met him for the first time, and it's obvious now.

I reach up, grab the gag from my mouth. Bud had warned me that he'd hurt me if I took it out, but he can't hurt me now.

'Dane, don't listen to him!'

Dane keeps his eyes trained on Bud, keeps his hand at his throat.

'You OK Harper? Did he hurt you? What happened to your chin?' My Daddy's voice is harsh but tender at the same time. I get the feeling that he's desperate to come to me, but there's no way he can.

'It wasn't him. Baby did it. They came to your apartment, Baby and Darlin'. They took me.'

'I had to give you away,' Bud says. 'It was the only safe thing to do. The only responsible thing to do. Then, soon as I was on the straight and narrow, as soon as I could, I tracked you down, and I saved you. Saved you from making the same mistakes you did.'

'He's not your parent, Dane!' I say. 'Margot's the only parent you've got, not this monster.'

'Who's Margot?' Bud says. Instantly, I know I've made a huge mistake.

'Harper, you're right. Bud, I can't let this continue. It's time for you to pay for your crimes. Whether you're my father or not doesn't matter. Far as I'm concerned, I don't have a father.'

'Dane, no, you're making a mista-'

But before he can finish his sentence, Dane pulls his hand back. For a horrible moment, I think I've just seen him kill Bud. It's only a moment later, when I see Dane smack the pommel of the knife into the side of Bud's temple that I can breathe a sigh of relief.

Bud's eyes close as he slips into unconsciousness.

The moment he's out cold, Dane springs into action. He runs to me, takes me in his arms, hugs me tight. My heart flutters, my body relaxes, he holds me up and I feel safe again.

'My darling Babygirl,' he whispers. 'I thought I was gonna lose you.' He strokes my hair, holds me tight. 'I'm never letting you out of my

CHAPTER TWENTY-FIVE

sight again.'

'I'm OK with that, Daddy,' I say. 'I'm seriously OK with that.'

Dane kisses the top of my head. 'We've got to move. I don't know how we're gonna get out of here, but if we don't get going, we're toast.'

'Frank, too.'

Dane looks over at Frank. 'He's still alive? What a tough motherfucker. He saved us, you know. Son of a bitch fucking sacrificed himself.' Dane heads over to Frank, and in an instant, he rips off his shirt, and ties it round Frank's leg.

I'm surprised to see the cling-film, wrapped around his arm, and the ink beneath. Seems like a lifetime ago that we were in Rock's tattoo shop. So much has happened, so much has changed.

'Caught a round in the leg. Don't think it hit anything too bad. Blood loss could be a fuck of a lot worse.'

'Do you think Bud is your dad?'

He stops for a second, looks at. 'I know he is,' he says, nodding. 'Soon as he said it, I felt the truth of it in my gut. I don't want it to be true, but it is.'

'What are you going to do about him?'

'I can't kill him.' He shakes his head. 'Thought I could, but I can't. Even before I knew he was my dad. He's done too much for me. I know that there's good in him. Only thing I can do is hand him over to the authorities. He has to pay for his crimes.'

'Hey, everything alright in there?' It's Baby's voice, outside the door.

Dane holds his finger to his lips, and I stand still, totally silent. Dane pads over next to the door, and motions towards me, showing me that I should stay where I am.

A moment later, the door swings open, and I see Baby standing there.

LUCKY MOON

'What the-' he starts, eyes fixed on me. Dane jumps him, pulling his arm across Baby's throat, tugging hard. Baby's eyes look like they're gonna pop out his head. Then a moment later, they close, and he's out like a light.

'We need to move,' Dane says. He looks down at the bodies in the room. 'I can only carry one of them, though. Fuck.'

'If we leave Frank, he'll die,' I say, tears welling in my eyes.

'If I leave Bud, he'll get away.' Dane counters.

He thinks for a moment, then lets out a shout of anguish. It's loud and angry — I've never heard him this pained.

'Fuck!' he cries. Then, to my relief, he stoops down and scoops Frank up. 'Come on, babe, we need to go. No more time left. Stay close to me, and if anyone says anything that sounds like it might get us into trouble, you run. I'll deal with the consequences.'

I nod, my heart going crazy with anxiety. I wish I was strong enough to carry Bud — but there's obviously no way. Dane grabs Bud's gun, and tucks it in his hand. At least we've got a weapon. That's something.

When we leave the room, the strange, chemical smell of this place hits even harder. I guess we're just hoping that we can get out of here without any of the Blood Fuckers seeing us. I'm so out of my depth and feel so useless.

'OK,' he says. 'We're gonna be heading through a big room full of workers cutting drugs. It's dark in there, and if we stick to the edges, we should be able to sneak out. Don't make eye-contact with anyone, don't do anything to draw attention to us.'

I nod. 'I'll do my best.'

'Baby, you're amazing. We're gonna get through this, I promise. And when this is all over, I'm gonna take you for the biggest fucking ice-cream you've ever seen in your life. Then, after that — swimming.

CHAPTER TWENTY-FIVE

Water slides, wave pools, the fucking works.'

He's smiling and I return his smile. The thought of doing normal stuff with Dane is so sweet that I can't help grinning, even in this shitty situation.

'Don't you think we should swim first, Daddy? Don't want to get a hurty tummy.'

He looks surprised. 'Damn. Didn't even think of that. My Daddy sense must be all frazzled by this madness.'

'Well, you have got my boss over your shoulder.'

'I guess you're right.' He looks suddenly serious. 'Right, Babygirl, are you ready for this?'

I kiss his cheek. 'I'm ready, Daddy.'

He pushes the door open. I wasn't prepared for how grim the sight is. There are rows of desks in the warehouse, dimly lit by desk lamps. Dozens of hungry-looking men, women and even children, are sitting at the desks. None of them look up at me as we start to walk through the space.

We move quick, and we don't look back, sticking to the shadows at the edges of the room, just like Dane said. We're in luck — there aren't any Blood Fuckers in here, and before too long, we're just a few paces from the door.

And then, when we're so close to freedom I can almost smell the fresh air, Frank lets out a long, protracted groan.

Dane drops down low, and I follow his lead, but a moment later, a blinding light snaps on, and it's trained straight on us.

'Don't fucking move.'

'Not you, Darlin',' Dane says, his voice tired and angry. 'Just when this fucking day couldn't get any damn worse.'

'Well, well, well,' Darlin' says, slinking her way down the steps, after us, 'looks like you nearly made it out of here.'

Next to her is Bud. There's blood down the side of his face from where Dane hit him with the knife, and he looks stunned still. But he's standing, and he's awake.

I grab hold of Dane's hand. I feel like our luck's about to run out.

Dane lifts the gun to point straight at Darlin'. 'Just let us go,' he says. 'No need to make this situation any worse than it already is.'

'I'm afraid that's not an option,' Bud says, coughing and spluttering. 'There's no way that you're getting out of here alive. Gotta defend our turf, Dane. You know the drill.'

Darlin' points her own gun — a small, shiny revolver — at us.

'Drop your fucking piece,' she says. 'Backup's coming for us. Any second.'

Sure enough, the front door opens, and a moment later, grunts stream through, all armed and angry.

'Is this it, Daddy?' I ask, my voice so quiet only Dane can hear me.

'Not quite,' he says. 'Got one more ace in the hole.' Then he shouts to Bud, 'Wait! I've got your missing drugs. Thirty grand's worth. You want that dope, you'll let Harper go. Do what you want with me.'

Bud grins a horrible grin. 'I don't give a shit about the money, Dane. All I care about is you.'

There's a horrible noise. But it's not a gun-shot. It's raw and it's wild and it's really loud, and it sounds like it's coming from everywhere all at once.

All the workers at the desks look around, scared, and the Blood Fuckers look left and right, trying to work out what's going on. The sound starts again, a low, powerful, mechanical rumble that builds and builds.

'Oh, you're in trouble now,' Dane says. 'I'd get out of here while

CHAPTER TWENTY-FIVE

you still can. Looks like the cavalry is finally here, Bud. And they're not gonna be happy to find you here.'

The sound is motorbikes. And lots of them. All revving their engines at the same time — a brutal symphony of pistons and spark plugs, of exhausts and gears.

'Everyone out!' Bud shouts. 'Take them out!'

But before anyone can move, there's another roar of motorbike engine, and a smash of glass, as a bike crashes straight through a floor to ceiling window. A moment later a bike smashes through a window on the other side. It's Rock and Hawk. More bikers start to stream through, and then, the shooting starts.

'Get down,' shouts Dane, 'and follow me!'

It's chaos. The workers scream and shout and stream for the exit, as Daddies MC and the Blood Fuckers tear each other to shreds. The Fuckers have no cover though, and within seconds, they realize that they're in a losing position, and they start to run, en-masse, for an exit at the back end of the room.

We're nearly out, and I look back to see Bud and Darlin' heading out with the rest of the gang. A couple of Blood Fuckers are on the ground, nursing wounds.

'Don't look,' commands Dane, as we finally head out of the warehouse. That's when the full scale of the situation hits me. There are dozens of Daddies MC members, queuing up to get into the warehouse.

And at the back, commanding the troops, is Ripper. When he sees Frank over Dane's shoulder, he runs immediately to us.

'Thank god you're OK,' Ripper says, looking at me.

'Frank's hurt,' I say, hoarse and scared.

Before Rip can have a look, there's a huge explosion, followed by shouts and even more confusion. I feel like I'm in a war-zone —

hopefully this will be the closest I ever come to something like that.

'Fuck,' Dane says. 'It's on fire.'

I look back, and see warm light spilling out from inside the warehouse. 'Daddy,' I say, 'I want to get away. I'm scared.'

He nods. 'Doc, can you do anything for Frank here?'

Ripper shakes his head. 'Need to get him to a hospital.' He pulls out a walkie talkie. 'And we need to call everyone out — don't want to lose anyone in that blaze. I'll take care of the clean-up, and you two head out.'

Dane nods. 'How did you know to come, Rip?'

Ripper looks grim. 'They got Babs and Titus. Soon as she didn't check in with me at five like she always does when she's staying away from home, I knew something was wrong.'

'Satan's Bud,' Dane says. 'Make sure that everyone knows.'

'You serious?'

'Never been more fucking serious, Rip.'

Ripper shakes his head, looks desperately sad. 'I knew something was wrong. Never did anything about it.'

'None of us did,' Dane replies.

'Come on now,' Ripper says. 'Get out of here. Your Little needs some love.'

That's when I remember, Dane said he loved me. He probably just said it in the heat of the moment. It barely seems important what with everything that's happened today. And yet, it's stuck in my head.

We make it back to Angeline, and I get up behind Dane. From somewhere nearby, I hear the whine of sirens as the cops make their way to the blaze. Somehow, pushing up against my Daddy like this, I feel a bizarre peace take hold of me. I can barely process what's happened today. I think it's going to be a while before I can.

CHAPTER TWENTY-FIVE

I nearly died. Dane nearly died. Frank nearly died.

'Honey,' Dane says, sliding the key into the ignition. 'I want you to know something. I meant what I said back there.' He turns, looks back at me. His face is full of complex emotion: sadness, pride, relief, intense, burning affection. 'I love you, Harper.'

It knocks the wind from me. Then, his kiss puts it back.

'I love you too,' I reply.

'Always and forever.'

'Always and forever.'

The bike starts. My heart beats. Life will never be the same again.

CHAPTER TWENTY-SIX

DANE
ONE MONTH LATER

'We're gonna be late!' Harper's voice in my ear is loud and clear, even though we're riding Angeline through mid-morning traffic.

'No fucking chance. I'm never gonna be late for one of these damn meetings ever again.' The helmet to helmet communication system is one of the best damn investments I ever met. Until I met Harper, I never thought that I'd have someone on the back of my bike often enough to make something like this worthwhile.

'Better hurry up then, Daddy!' she says, giggling manically.

'Since when did you turn into such a damn speed demon?' I ask, dodging between a bus and a pickup truck.

'Since I met you, of course.'

We're on our way to The Milk Shed for one of the important days in the history of the club. For the first time ever, the boys are voting on a new president for Daddies MC. And, with a little luck, I should be able to make it to the bar on time.

Provided absolutely nothing goes wrong.

'Watch out!' yelps Harper, as I narrowly avoid a cyclist.

'Idiot was in the wrong lane,' I grunt.

'Don't hit cyclists!' Harper says. 'I don't want you falling in love with anyone else!'

I can't help but laugh. 'As if I could,' I say. She squeezes me a little harder. I love how affectionate she is with me. Fuck it, I love everything about her.

'Nearly there,' I say.

'I'm excited!'

'For the vote?'

'No, silly. For play time!'

It's only been a month since the fire that destroyed the Blood Fuckers drugs operation, but a *lot* has changed at Daddies MC. Without Bud in charge, the soul of the club has changed. There's a lot less of an emphasis on macho posturing, and much more of an emphasis placed on building a nurturing, positive environment for Littles to flourish in.

And no Little has been flourishing more than my Harper.

The transformation in her has been unreal. I don't know whether it's the structure, the affirmations, or just getting to know a heck of a lot other Littles, but it feels as though any residual feelings of shame she had about who she is have just disappeared.

And I couldn't be happier.

'I should have known,' I say, shaking my head. 'Who cares who's gonna set the agenda for the club when there's pool to play and arcades to win the high-score for.'

'You really get me, Daddy,' she chuckles.

There have been other surprising benefits to having Bud out of the picture.

In the showdown at the BF warehouse, he told me that without the income from the illicit activities that he was involved in, our club would have fallen apart.

That is *not* the case. In fact, when me, Rip and Hawk sat down and looked at club finances with Parker, the club accountant, it became clear as fucking crystal that Bud had been siphoning money away from all the businesses. When we stopped all the standing orders and canceled his credit card payments, all of a sudden, things started to look pretty damn rosy.

CHAPTER TWENTY-SIX

I spent some of my extra money to buy some new arcade machines, which Harper promptly got addicted to. Whenever we're at The Milk Shed these days, she can generally be found trying to get Roxy to come play with her, or trying to beat Babs' high score on Donkey Kong.

'You think Ripper's gonna be voted in?' Harper says.

'Oh, so you *do* care about the vote.' I'm grinning, but I try to keep my voice stern. Don't want Harper to know how cute I find it when she gets involved with club politics.

'Course I care,' she says. 'And I don't want Marcus winning. That'd be terrible!'

Marcus is one of the old guard of the club. He was a good friend of Bud's, and if he took over as club president, things might not go so good for Daddies MC. He's definitely not shy of breaking the law, and I've got a feeling that we might even have something of a civil war on our hands if he does win the vote.

'I don't think he's got enough support,' I say. I hope that I'm right.

Course, none of us have heard anything from Bud since the night in that warehouse. The cops arrested a bunch of the Blood Fuckers. Rock's contact inside the LAPD said that the force was pretty fucking happy with us. They'd been trying to bust the Fuckers for months, and when we took apart their warehouse, it was like an early Christmas present for them.

Sadly, Bud got away. As did Baby and Darlin'. Most of the guys think they probably skipped town, and I'm inclined to agree. But at the same time, I feel most certain that it's not the last we've seen of them.

The more I find out about what Bud was doing, the more convinced I become that the guy — my father — is a sociopath. He was in abusive relationships with a couple of the regular Littles at the nightclub he ran. Not healthy BDSM relationships. Like, very bad, controlling-type affairs.

Someone like that doesn't just leave a club he's been building his whole life, never to be seen again.

We eventually arrive at the bar with a few minutes to spare.

'Told you,' I say, as we slip off the bike.

Harper's wearing a powder-pink helmet, over the top of her brand-new bike leathers. She looks ridiculously cute in the tight-fitting outfit, and as sexy as hell to boot. When she takes that helmet off, revealing her gorgeous dark red hair and light-pink cheeks, I feel lust stir in my gut.

I pull my own helmet off, feel the cool air on my face.

'We made it,' she says, before she whoops as I circle my hands round her waist.

'Never mind that,' I say, pressing my lips into hers. 'Any spare time is make-out time, far as I'm concerned.'

I feel her smile as we kiss again. I ran my hands over her butt, pulling her body in close to me again. 'Fuck you smell good,' I growl. 'Leather and candy. Who'd have thought it'd be such a killer combination?'

'Leather and candy,' she says, musing over the words. 'That could be the name of the film they make of our love. Coming to a theater near you!'

'Nah,' I say. 'I'd just call our story *Harper*.'

She grins. 'You couldn't. Especially not if it was a novel. Everyone knows that you've got to name romance stories after the main male characters.'

I grunt out a laugh. 'Who would buy a book called Dane?'

'I would.' She pushes herself up against me. 'And I'd definitely kiss a guy called Dane.'

'Fuck! Will you two, just get a damn room! It's been a month. Shouldn't the honeymoon period be over by now?' Rock's voice is

CHAPTER TWENTY-SIX

unmistakable, as is his grumpy attitude.

'Ah, the voice of jealousy,' Dane says, turning to face his old friend.

'Yeah, yeah,' growls Rock. 'Take it you heard about me and Lisa?'

'I'm sorry,' Harper says. 'I really liked he-'

'No, you didn't!' Rock replies, smiling. 'You thought she was terrible, just like everyone else. And you were right.'

'Hey,' Harper says, 'I've got something to make you feel better.'

'Is it a sister?' Rock asks.

'Watch it,' I caution him.

'No harm in asking.'

Harper opens the pannier on the side of Angeline, and pulls out a box. 'These are fresh as can be. Don't tell anyone that you're getting an extra one, or there could be a riot.'

She opens the box, and takes out a fresh-baked cinnamon bun.

'Should a big, burly biker really eat one of those?' Rock asks, as he takes the pastry from Harper.

'Don't worry, Rock, we won't tell anyone,' I say. 'Your precious bad boy reputation's safe.'

He takes a bite and his eyes widen. 'Holy fuck if that ain't the tastiest damn thing I've ever put in my mouth.'

'Right, come on,' I say. 'Let's get this meeting going.'

*

The Milk shed is packed. It's way busier than normal, and there isn't even any music on the juke box.

The Littles are all in the playroom at the moment, leaving just the Daddies who are casting votes in today's decision.

That's something that I hope Ripper will change, when he's made

President of the club. Feels so archaic to me that our Littles — who are so invested in the Motorcycle Club — don't get a say in the way club decisions are taken.

There's a low murmur of discussion in the room, and the atmosphere is electric. Finally, when it feels like everyone's naturally waiting for the proceedings to begin, I stand up.

'Alright. We all know why we're here. A month ago, we discovered that our founder, Bud Spence, was a snake. He threatened our club, our lives, and worst of all, our Littles.'

Grunts of agreement roll around the room.

'It's been long enough now. We need to elect a new president, to take us into the future. So, I wanna kick things off by nominating Ripper. He's a smart, fair, forward-thinking man who'll do well by the club.'

I nod over at Rip. He's got a funny look on his face, but doesn't say anything.

'Anyone else got any nominations to make?'

A hand goes up. It's Curtis, one of the old boys of the club. No prizes for guessing who he's gonna nominate.

'Curtis?'

'I nominate Marcus. He's tough, and he don't take no prisoners. He'll do whatever it takes to protect the club. Help us thrive.'

There are a few grunts of approval, none of them louder than Marcus'.

'Thank you, Curtis. Anyone else?'

To my surprise, Ripper's hand shoots up.

'Uh, Rip? What's the matter?'

He stands. 'Everyone here knows that *you're* the best choice for president, Dane.'

CHAPTER TWENTY-SIX

I feel shock in my gut. Me and Ripper have talked about this. He knows that I don't wanna do this. I'm not ready. I'm not worthy.

'I dunno,' I say. 'I feel li-'

'We need someone to unite this club,' Ripper says. 'Someone who understands the good intentions Bud had when he set Daddies MC up.' There are a few quiet cheers of agreement from the guys. 'But more than that, we need someone who knows that things need to change. Someone who can help us re-focus. And there's no-one better placed than our vice-president.'

It's not that I haven't thought about it before. And I *do* have big ideas for where I wanna take the club. Focus on protecting vulnerable Littles and working with local community groups who need help. I wanna focus on our legitimate business, too.

More than that, I want to build up a true relationship with the local police. Prove to them that we're not a menace, that we went to be protectors, not intimidate local folks.

'What do you say, boss?' Hawk says. 'You gonna let us nominate you?'

'Fine.' I say. 'But I'm not happy you haven't discussed this with me.'

'We tried, you stubborn ass — this is the only way to prove to you that the whole club's behind you.'

I groan. He's right of course.

'Whatever,' I say. 'Let's just get on with the damn vote.'

So, we vote. And I fucking win.

CHAPTER TWENTY-SEVEN

HARPER

'It's a landslide! The biggest election victory in the history of Daddies MC!'

'Harper,' grunts Dane, laughing a little, 'it's the only vote in the history of the club.'

Everyone around the table laughs.

'So, I'm right!' I giggle.

Dane kisses my cheek. 'That's right, Baba,' he says, 'you keep telling yourself that.'

We're around one of the biggest tables in The Milk Shed, and everyone's in celebration mode. For Rock and Hawk, that means whiskeys. Ripper is sipping at a frosty beer, and Babs has a white wine spritzer.

'So how does it feel to be the first lady of Daddies MC?' Ripper asks.

'First Little?' I ask, to a couple of laughs.

'Right.'

'Feels amazing,' I say. 'Although I don't feel as though I deserve it.'

'Bullshit,' says Dane. 'You've been through hell. Course you fucking deserve it. Thought we'd been through this sweetheart — no putting yourself down.'

'I know,' I say. 'I just mean — I'm so new to all this. Feels like I've walked into...' I look at the faces of the people I've grown to love in such a crazy short time. 'Feels like I've walked into a whole family.'

Babs leans over, strokes my arm.

'I've got my mom,' I say, looking at Babs. 'Course my Daddy.' Dane winks at me. 'There are my two shit-head brothers.'

'No cussin', sis,' Rock says.

'I'mma let you off on this occasion,' Dane laughs. 'The swearing was too damn accurate to get too angry about.'

'What about me?' Ripper asks.

'Uncle Rip, of course,' I. 'The fun cool uncle that you know is gonna show you all the best places to go drinking around town.'

'I'll drink to that,' Rip grins, lifting his beer to his lips.

'Cool Uncle Rip,' Babs says. 'Gotta funny ring to it, Daddy.'

'I'd be a very good uncle,' Rip says, playfully.

'I bet you would,' Babs replies. 'Not sure I'd make such a good momma though.'

'Only cause you seem so wise and smart,' I say. Then, I bite my lip. 'And because you can't even come close to my high-score on Donkey Kong.'

It feels so good to laugh with all these wonderful people. There's just one person missing.

Roxy walks up to us, looks at each of us in turn. Obviously, her eyes linger on Hawk for a little longer than they do on everyone else. I really like Roxy — feels like she's got hidden depths. But she's always a little reserved with me, like she's unsure about something, or she's hiding her true self.

'Hey guys, I've got someone at reception, asking for Harper. Haven't seen her before.'

Dane looks confused.

'Hope you don't mind,' I say. 'But I invited Felicity. I feel like I'm finally ready to show this side of myself to her. She's open-minded, and she's super-nice. I think you're all gonna like her.'

'I don't mind at all,' he says, but there's a look of concern in his eyes. 'I'm glad that you wanna share that part of your life with me. I'm

CHAPTER TWENTY-SEVEN

excited to meet her.'

'But...?' I say, my voice a little unsteady.

'I just... there's something we've gotta do today.'

'What?' I ask. I wrack my brains — can't think of anything. We visited Margot the day before yesterday, so it can't be that.

'It's just something,' he says, looking at his watch. 'Should still have time though. Sorry to make you think about time.'

'No problem,' I say, but I am a little disappointed. Nothing like a deadline to take the excitement out of a social occasion.

'So, should I bring her in?' Roxy says.

'Yes please!' I say.

I've been through so much recently, so many objectively terrifying and life-changing experiences. Yet somehow, the thought of finally coming clean to Felicity about my life, about who I really am. It's about the scariest thing I've ever done.

She walks through the front door of the bar, and looks from side to side, as Roxy leads her across the room. I just know that her writer's brain is going berserk at the moment — taking in all the details of the place, getting ready to commit it all to page.

'Hey,' she says, as she comes near.

'Hey,' says everyone around the table.

'Wow!' Felicity replies. 'What a welcome! I'm so excited to meet you all. This place is amazing.'

'Flick,' I say. 'This is Dane.'

Dane holds out his hand to my best friend and they shake. I've shown Flick a picture of Dane before, but I think she's a little overwhelmed by just how imposing and intimidating he is. And not just him, either. There's Rock and Hawk to contend with.

'Don't worry sugar,' Dane says. 'We don't bite.'

'I do,' Rock says, practically snarling.

'Don't listen to him,' I say. 'He's a pussy cat.'

'More like a cougar,' he says.

'You're an older woman who likes to prey on young men?' Felicity says, her eyes twinkling playfully. Everyone laughs, except for Rock, who pulls out his comb, and drags it across his hair.

'I like her,' Ripper says. 'Can I get you a drink, sweetheart?'

'Cosmopolitan?'

'You bet your ass I am, but what can I get you to drink.'

Everyone groans.

'Fine, fine, I'll get to the bar. Honestly, young people these days wouldn't know a good joke if it came up and slapped 'em in the face.'

'So,' Felicity says when we're all settled. 'You said that you had something important you wanted to tell me.'

I breathe in deep. 'I do. It's gonna be kind of a lot. So I'm gonna go back a long way. But I need to tell you. I can't keep lying about who I am. Dane helped me with that.'

She grins, then leans in, whispers to me. 'He's good for you, any idiot can tell that.'

'OK,' I say. 'Promise you won't judge me.'

'You got it,' she replies.

I breathe in deep, open my mouth, and let the truth fly free.

*

'You have to be honest. How angry would you be if I wrote a film script about this?'

'I knew it!' I laugh. 'I knew you'd want to mine my life for your own personal gain.'

CHAPTER TWENTY-SEVEN

'Let me drink your sweet tears,' Flick says, taking pretend sips from her clenched fingers. I've no doubt that Felicity is only joking about this — there's no way that a film about Littles and their biker Daddies would ever get made, is there?

'Who would you get to play me in a film?' Dane says.

'Hmmm,' Felicity says. 'Now there's a question. You know what? This is gonna sound kinda weird. But, you're kinda like a scarred, badass version of Cary Grant.'

Dane laughs so hard beer almost sprays out his nose. 'Cary fucking Grant? He's dead! You planning on necromancing his damn corpse out of the ground for one final, triumphant performance?'

'Holy shit,' says Flick, 'that's an even better idea for a film. You guys are a damn gold mine!'

'What about me?' Rock asks. 'Johnny Depp? You know. Young Johnny Depp. Hot Johnny Depp. Johnny Depp before he went all… questionable.'

'I was thinking Steve Buscemi,' Felicity replies, to hoots of laughter from around the table. 'You know, a weirder looking Steve Buscemi.'

I've got this feeling — because I know how Felicity gets — that even though she's being all mean and viper-tongued — that she might actually have a bit of a thing for Rock. And there's no question that he's got a thing for her.

Hmm. This could get interesting.

'Hey, I'll take that,' he says. 'Buscemi's a fucking genius. You see him in Reservoir Dogs? A sensational performance.'

Suddenly, an alarm sounds from Dane's phone. He grabs it out his pocket.

'Sweetheart,' he says, 'we gotta go.'

'Do we have to, Daddy?' I whine. 'I'm having so much fun.'

'I know, I know. I'm having fun, too. But I promise, you won't want to miss this. And there'll be plenty of time for fun in the future.'

'It's OK, hun,' Flick says. 'You go. I'm gonna stick around here for a while, have another couple drinks. This is too much fun!'

'Uggghhhh,' I groan. 'I know. I wanna stay. This is so unfair!'

'Come on now, don't be a brat,' Dane warns. 'Or you won't sit well for a day. Let's not turn what should be a really exciting day into something else.'

I know that Daddy's serious about his punishment threats. He's not disciplined me too many times over the past month, but when he did, he didn't hold back.

Course, that didn't stop me enjoying it.

Plus, did he say that this should be an exciting day? What exactly are we doing?

I love surprises — but I'm not gonna let Daddy know that of course.

'Fine,' I say, crossing my arms. 'I'll follow your dang rules. But I'm not gonna like it.'

'Good enough,' Dane says, holding out my helmet. 'Let's hit the road.'

CHAPTER TWENTY-EIGHT

DANE

We turn the corner onto Spring street and I start to brake, pulling Angeline off the street and onto the sidewalk. We come to a stop just underneath a huge piece of street art: a beautiful woman's face, light in white gold, staring at Los Angeles like a benevolent protector.

'Fancy!' Harper says. 'What are we doing Downtown?'

'You like it round here?' I ask. I'm nervous, but I'm trying to keep it out of my voice. If Harper knew how much effort and planning had gone into what I'm about to show her, she'd be just as nervous as me. Knowing her, she'd be even more nervous.

'Course I do!' she says. 'Ohh, you taking me for a fancy drink somewhere? I heard there was a really cool new cocktail bar round her.'

She pauses for a moment, looks at me with a quizzical expression.

'What's going on, Daddy? You're being all weird.'

'You noticed?'

I look at my watch. Where is he? He's meant to be here already. Fucking clown, I knew he couldn't be trusted not to fuck this up.

Just as I'm about to blurt out what's going on, there's a small cough from behind me. Sounds like someone's clearing their throat.

'Frank!' Harper squeals.

'Hey guys, good to see ya.'

Frank looks different. Since Ripper saved his life a month ago, it feels like he's been given a whole new lease of life. He's lost weight — it's only been a month, but he looks ten years younger. And there's a keenness in his eye that Harper tells me she's never seen before.

'Good to see you too!' Harper runs up to him and gives him a huge cuddle. 'You're looking so good!' she says.

'It's the whole-food plant-based diet I'm on,' he says, smiling wide.

'Whole-food?' Harper says.

'Plant-based?' I echo.

'Sounds like hell, doesn't it?' he says. 'But honestly, I've never been happier. Had to buy a whole new wardrobe.'

It's not been all sunshine and lollipops for Frank, of course. The LAPD took a pretty close look at all his business dealings after the fire at the warehouse. He proved he was being extorted, luckily enough, but he still lost his business. Without the money coming in from the Blood Fuckers, he just couldn't keep it going.

'I'm happy for you,' I say. 'But if you try to feed me even a single piece of tofu, I'll go berserk.'

'Tofu isn't a whole food,' he says, shaking his head. 'Far too unhealty for me.'

'Get out of it!' Harper says, punching his arm. 'You're terrible.'

'Hey,' Frank says, 'I've got something for you. Dane and me have been looking for a while, and I think we've finally got the perfect place.'

'What do you mean?' Harper says. 'Perfect place?'

Frank gestures at the unit underneath the graffiti of the woman's face. Harper look confused, even though she sees the 'Shop To Let' sign in the window.

'I don't get it.'

Frank takes something outta his pocket — a small, shiny key.

'This is for you,' he says. 'Originally, I was gonna buy this place, expand Superstar Frosting with a location Downtown, but it makes more sense that you would be the one to take on this exciting new opportunity.'

'I don't-'

CHAPTER TWENTY-EIGHT

'Harper,' I say. 'This place is for you. It's gonna be your bakery.'

Her eyes widen. She looks frantically from Frank to me and back again.

'Is this a joke?'

'No joke,' I say.

'Absolutely not,' Frank replies.

'But why?'

'Your business plan has really come together recently, don't you think? We've costed everything together, from ingredients to staff, to marketing. But there's no point in any of that if you don't have a damn location to run everything from. And I don't think that your studio apartment kitchen is big enough, do you?'

'I can't believe this is happening!' Harper says. I don't think I've ever seen her smile this wide before.

'You deserve it,' says Frank. 'But don't think I'm doing this from the goodness of my heart. No — I want something.'

'What could I possibly have that you want?' Harper asks.

'A job,' he says. 'Think about it. I could be some kind of health consultant. Plus, I haven't done any baking for years, I'd like to get back in the kitchen. Need to re-learn my trade.'

'Are you joking?' Harper asks. 'You saved our lives. Of course I'll give you a job.'

'Whoa whoa,' I say. 'Now don't be hasty. This business is gonna fall within the Daddies MC business portfolio. I need to make sure that all our staff members uphold the values of the organization.'

Frank laughs. 'I'll do my best, sir.'

'So, this is all part of the club, too?' Harper says, with disbelief. She's been desperate to have some kind of official recognition from the club. At the moment, it's just the guys who have a say in the running of the organization. It's something I want to gently change, but it's gonna take time.

'Yep,' I say. 'You're not quite an official club member, but this is about as close as you can get right now. But I'm gonna work on it, I promise.'

'We should start our own club,' Frank says. 'Although what's that old saying? Oh yeah — I don't want to join any club that would have me as a member!'

I'm glad that Frank could be here for this. There's something incredibly symbolic about him passing the keys to Harper, about her knowing that she's got the trust and expertise of the older generation backing her up. I think if he wasn't here, showing her his belief, she might not have accepted the offer.

'Right, I'm gonna leave you two love birds to look around the property. I'm available for help with kitting the place out, and getting it up and running. Anything you need, I'm your guy.'

He shakes my hand, then embraces Harper again. He's like a different man. I guess he's found himself again.

'So, you wanna go check out your new bakery?' I ask.

'There's literally nothing I want to do more!' Harper squeals.

My nerves haven't gone. Because the thing I'm dreading the most hasn't happened yet.

CHAPTER TWENTY-NINE

HARPER

We cross the busy street, and I'm so excited I'm skipping, dancing through the cars. I can't believe my Daddy has done this for me. He's given me everything — confidence, hope, and now, a whole new life.

I wish I could give him something in return.

We approach the front door of the building and I press myself up to the huge windows. This place is gonna be an amazing bakery. I wonder what it was before. Looks like maybe it was a deli, or some kinda restaurant, because there's a counter that's got a couple old display fridges next to it.

'Can we go in?' I ask, grabbing Dane's hand and looking up into his handsome face.

'Well, seeing as it's your name on the lease, I reckon that might be OK.'

I squeal with delight and slide the key into the lock. Takes me a second to open it — the door's a little stiff.

'I'm gonna have to learn all this place's little quirks,' I giggle. 'Come on, Mr. Squeaky Door, give up your secrets.'

'Think the only secret is that this door needs a good squirt of WD40 so that it obeys its new mistress.'

'I'm the mistress, huh?'

'That's right. But don't forget who your Daddy is,' he grins.

'Never,' I say, curling myself round his big body. I love the way he smells. I love the way he feels.

'So,' Dane says. 'Can you see yourself in here? Managing a team? Managing Frank?'

The thought is seriously daunting. My whole life I've barely been able to manage myself. Now I might have to actually tell other people what to do. It's nuts.

'I dunno,' I say.

'Is that self-doubt I hear in your voice?'

'Maybe.' I say. 'Just a smidgen.'

'You got a case of impostor syndrome?'

'What's that?' I say, wrinkling my nose.

'It's when you feel like you're out of your depth. Like you've been asked to do something that you don't feel capable of doing. Like you're an impostor, pretending to be someone you're not.'

That's exactly how I feel. 'Honestly, I've kind of felt like that my whole life.'

Dane nods. 'Everyone gets it. Fuck, I've had it. Any time anyone tells me I've done a good job. Or that I'm worth a damn.'

'You get it, too? You're the most insanely confident person I've ever met.'

He snorts. 'You gotta be kidding me. I don't know what I'm doing basically all the time. How do you think I feel, being asked to be club president?'

'Like you were born to do it?'

He shakes his head. 'Nope. Like there's no way I can do a good job.' Then he reaches out to me, takes hold of my hand. 'But you know what? I think that's *why* I'm gonna do a good job. Because I've got a hunger to learn. A hunger to do well. And I know that if I fail, my ass is on the line.'

Eek. I guess my ass is on the line.

'I hope I don't mess this up,' I say. 'Hope I don't do crazy stuff like try to deliver cakes when I'm ill.'

CHAPTER TWENTY-NINE

'Hey, that wasn't your fault.'

'I know, I just... I hope that I don't ruin this for you.'

He takes both my hands in his, gently strokes my fingers. 'Sweetheart. My darling Babygirl. You won't. You can't. Look — it's like this. Everything we do, we do for the first time. Each new discussion. Each new relationship. Each new fucking cake we bake. There's no practice. No dry runs. No take backs.'

I nod.

'But we keep going. We make mistakes, we learn, we grow. We get humiliated, we get over it. We don't let our mistakes define us. We don't let our past rule us. Because everything in the past is gone, and everything ahead of us is pure, golden opportunity.'

For a moment, he looks as though he's considering something. Then, before I know what's going on, he crouches, down, onto one knee.

'What the-'

'Harper,' he says. 'I've got impostor syndrome, because of you. I feel like there's no way I deserve someone as good, as pure, as perfect as you.'

As he talks, my hands start to tremble. Then my arms. Then my chest. Then my whole body is shaking like there's an earthquake going on.

'When you came into my life, I was an angry man, who only cared about my club. But I didn't have a heart. You became that heart, Harper. From the first moment I saw you, I knew that you were my future. But I need your help. I need you to help me cure this impostor syndrome. I need you to marry me.'

He takes a simple black box from his pocket, and opens it for me to see. Inside, there isn't a ring. There are two.

'Always felt kinda old-fashioned for just a woman to wear an engagement ring,' he says.

I'm trying to form sentences in my mind, trying to work out just what it is that I'm gonna say, but the words keep getting caught in my throat. 'So I got one for each of us,' he continues.

He picks out the smaller of the two, holds it up in the light. Inside, there's something engraved.

Dane's Little Girl.

I pick up the other one, look inside.

Harper's Daddy Dom.

I don't say a word, and neither does he. But together, at exactly the same moment, I slip the ring over his finger, and he does the same to me.

Then, when I feel the cool gold against my skin, I finally say, 'Of course I'll marry you, Daddy. You're everything to me.'

He surges upward, wrapping his arms around me, lifting me.

I hug him and he finds my lips, pushing hard into me as I push back. Now it does feel like a dream. One I never want to wake up from.

This kiss is different, like no other. He swallows me up, like a tiny snack, but at the same time, I'm devouring him, too. Like our lives are mixing, our essences combining.

'I've been so nervous,' he pants.

'I love you,' I reply. 'You're perfect.'

'Got something to show you,' he grunts, each of his words rushed, all his movements deliberate. He carries me across the open space of my new bakery, pushing open a swing door.

'Oh my!' I say. It's beautiful. He's set a space up for us. There's a pile of rugs on the floor, and flickering candles light the intimate space.

'It's your den,' he says. 'A little space for you. It's not much, but until your nursery is built at my place-'

'You're building a nursery for me?'

CHAPTER TWENTY-NINE

'Course,' he grins. 'Can't have you stay at mine without somewhere to relax in Little Space. What kind of Daddy would I be if I didn't provide that.'

'You're the best Daddy ever!' I say, kissing him again. 'And you're gonna be the best damn husband ever.'

'Hey,' he says, 'that sounded like a curse word to me.'

'Oh no!' I say. 'I was so excited, I totally forgot! Oh Daddy, please.'

'You know my stance on cursing,' he says.

Oh, this is so unfair. So cruel! 'Daddy I'm sorry!' I say, pleading.

'I don't want to hear it,' he says.

'What are you gonna do.'

'That's for me to know,' he says. Then he puts me down. 'Now turn round and spread your hands against that wall.'

I do as he asks, walking over to the wall, pushing my palms against it.

'Good girl. Now whatever happens, I don't want you to look back. Eyes forward.'

I nod. 'You're gonna spank me, aren't you?'

No reply. I'm desperate to look round, but I don't — I keep my eyes straight ahead, watching the dancing shadows the candles make on the bare wall.

A moment later, I feel Dane's hands on my pants, before he tugs them down.

'I bought something else for you,' he says. 'Something that I was gonna share with you later on. But you've given me no choice. I'm gonna have to use it on you right now.'

I gulp. *Use it on me?*

Dane's fingers dip under the waistband of my panties, before he pulls them down my legs. I feel the cool air on my pussy, which is already wet and hot with lust.

'What are you going to do?' I pant.

'You'll find out soon enough,' he growls. 'Let this be a lesson to you, sweetheart — Daddy means business.'

I wince as I feel something push against my pussy. It feels smooth and cool, and Dane pushes it gently between my lips. I moan with pleasure as he pushes it further in, and sigh as he slowly draws it out.

'Are you ready?' he asks, his voice trembling.

'Uh-huh,' I nod.

There's a quiet click, and then the most intense pleasure starts to radiate from my pussy as a ferocious buzzing vibration courses through my body.

'Oh my God,' I say. 'It's so intense.' I bite my lip. The sensation is insane — it feels like my legs are melting, like I'm going to collapse.

'You're gonna take it,' Dane says. 'Or there'll be double discipline later.'

'Yes Daddy,' I whine. 'I can take it.'

He slides the vibrator in and out, and I throw my head back with my eyes closed, clenching my teeth as the ecstasy builds in me. I rub my knees together, squirming like crazy, desperately trying to stay upright.

'Good Girl,' Dane says. 'You're doing great.'

He slides the nub up, over my wet clit, and I gasp with surprise and delight. 'Oh no,' I say, 'I'm gonna come.'

'Wait,' he says. 'You come when I tell you, and not a second before.'

'But I don't kn-'

'You can do it,' he commands.

And then, I feel it, his cock, the unmistakable size of it, the power of it, pushing into my hungry pussy as he slips the vibrator over my clit, again and again, and then, when he's filled me up, when he's balls deep

CHAPTER TWENTY-NINE

and I'm groaning with pleasure and discomfort, he pulls in close to my ear and whispers, hoarse and commanding, 'Now you come for me.'

Relief floods my body as I let go, let everything go: my fear, my doubt, everything. The rush of pleasure tugs me upwards, pulls me into a whole new world of ecstasy, as my hot pussy grips my lover's cock, and our two hearts beat as one.

'Daddy,' I moan, 'that was… unbelievable.'

'Believe it,' he says. 'And believe this, too.'

He drops the vibrator, grips my arms, pulls me back, and I feel his cock push further into me as I gasp and he starts to drill into me, like a machine. He pounds me from behind, grunting with each thrust, and then spins me round.

'Put it back in me,' I beg.

He pulls me close, lifts a leg, and slots himself straight back in, so smooth and confident and in control. He licks his lips as we look at each other, he holds my gaze as he fucks me raw and hard, shoving my ass up against the wall, pushing himself ferociously in and out.

'This is where I belong,' he growls, 'with you.'

'Right here,' I say, reaching down, gripping the shaft of his cock as it surges into me. 'With me,' I say, rubbing my clit. He moves his hand down, pushes on the center of my pleasure. I whimper. 'I can't take any more. I'm gonna catch on fire.'

'Then we'll both fucking burn.' He kisses me hard, pushing his tongue in deep, and he pauses, grinding his cock deep into me, rubbing his body against my pussy, shooting his fingers over my clit.

This time, when I come, for a moment I feel as though my senses are leaving me — like I can't hear, I can't see — all I can do is feel, as his cock erupts in me, painting my insides, making me laugh and cry all at the same time.

LUCKY MOON

And as we lie there, still attached, one perfect creature with two hearts, two minds, I know that this is my place, and this is my Daddy. And I'm his. Forever.

* * *

Thanks for reading! Hope you enjoyed my novel! If you did, don't forget to review it on Amazon. Oh, and join my mailing list for exclusive news and conten and plenty of fun surprises. Lucky x

NEXT IN SERIES

ROCK

Sometimes a good girl needs a bad Daddy...

FELICITY
There's no way he's good for me.
A whiskey-drinking, bare-knuckle-fighting, tattoo artist.
As s*xy as he is dangerous, as gruff as he is talented.
Rock is trouble.
And he's a Daddy Dom.
He'd never be interested in a vanilla girl like me.
So why can't I get him out of my head?
I should be focusing on my writing career.
I should be doing my job.
But Rock's under my skin.
Only question is: is it gonna be permanent?

ROCK
I want her so f*cking bad.
Ever since the first time I say her.
She's all I can think about.
Her body. Her fiery mouth.
I know she's too good for me.
But that doesn't mean I can get her out of my head.
I've got problems.
Demons from my past, threatening everything.
But when they start to threaten Felicity, nothing will stop me.
Time for me to fight for what I love.

MORE FROM LUCKY MOON

MC DADDIES
DANE
ROCK
HAWK

STANDALONE NOVELS
DADDY'S PROMISE
PLEASE DADDY

LITTLE RANCH SERIES
DADDY'S FOREVER GIRL
DADDY'S SWEET GIRL
DADDY'S PERFECT GIRL

MOUNTAIN DADDIES SERIES
TRAPPED WITH DADDY
LOST WITH DADDY
SAVED BY DADDY
STUCK WITH DADDY
TRAINED BY DADDY
GUARDED BY DADDY

DDLG MATCHMAKER SERIES
DADDY'S LITTLE BRIDE
DADDY'S LITTLE REBEL
DADDY'S LITTLE DREAM

BEST LITTLE FRIENDS SERIES
DADDY DOCTOR
DADDY BODYGUARD
DADDY BILLIONAIRE

SUGAR DADDY CLUB SERIES
PLATINUM DADDY
CELEBRITY DADDY
DIAMOND DADDY
CHAMPAGNE DADDY

Printed in Great Britain
by Amazon